A
DARKNESS
OF
GIANTS

Books by J. Allan Bosworth

For Young People

A BIRD FOR PETER
VOICES IN THE MEADOW
WHITE WATER, STILL WATER
ALL THE DARK PLACES
A WIND NAMED ANNE
A DARKNESS OF GIANTS

Novels

SPEED DEMON
THE LONG WAY NORTH

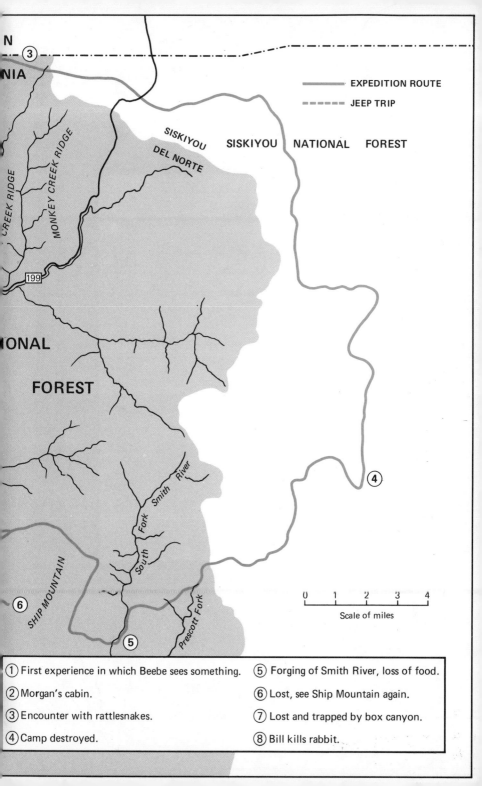

N

③

NIA

CREEK RIDGE

MONKEY CREEK RIDGE

199

SISKIYOU

DEL NORTE

SISKIYOU   NATIONAL   FOREST

——— EXPEDITION ROUTE

------- JEEP TRIP

IONAL

FOREST

④

Smith River

South Fork

SHIP MOUNTAIN

⑥

⑤

Prescott Fork

0   1   2   3   4
Scale of miles

① First experience in which Beebe sees something.

② Morgan's cabin.

③ Encounter with rattlesnakes.

④ Camp destroyed.

⑤ Forging of Smith River, loss of food.

⑥ Lost, see Ship Mountain again.

⑦ Lost and trapped by box canyon.

⑧ Bill kills rabbit.

A
DARKNESS
OF
GIANTS

J. Allan Bosworth

Doubleday & Company, Inc.
Garden City, New York   1972

Library of Congress Catalog Card Number 79–180062
Copyright © 1972 by J. Allan Bosworth
All Rights Reserved
Printed in the United States of America
First Edition

A
DARKNESS
OF
GIANTS

1.

He could not see the ceiling in the dark, but Greg Anders stared at it just the same, anxious and wondering. For all his trying, there were no comforting answers to be found in that inverted well of blackness, and yet neither could he turn away from it or close his eyes. And it was almost two o'clock . . . they would have to start out in a matter of hours.

The Six Rivers *Sentinel* had announced the expedition on the front page yesterday. By now, he knew the words well. In part, it said: *On a wilderness trek that could take them a hundred miles or more, the three young men hope to find and photograph one of the legendary creatures called Bigfoot.*

Greg threw his pillow across the room and sat up to groan. *Bigfoot,* for crying out loud! *Find* and *photograph* . . . even to glimpse one of those creatures would be remarkable. They were like ghosts in the

1

forests . . . shadows living in a world of shadows. They had been seen by rare chance. But to make a deliberate search . . . well, *hope* in this case was a brave and foolish word.

He had gone to the *Sentinel* to ask James Beverly for the photographer's position that would be open in a month. And, at first, the interview seemed to go well. His being eighteen had not mattered, and the editor had liked his portfolio. But then, leaning back, the man said, "Ninety-nine per cent of the job, here, is taking dull pictures . . . you know, the mayor shaking hands with somebody, Rotary Club elections, and so on. But it's the other one per cent that has to be considered . . . the kind of news event that happens suddenly and on its own terms. You can't pose it as you would a pretty girl. Sometimes, the photographer must shoot instinctively and just once to catch a moment that won't come again. I'm sorry. But since you seem best at portraits, why not try Geary's Studio? The old man might need an assistant." And with that, it had fallen apart. . . .

Later, Greg had seen that failing on his first try was hardly a disaster. But he had been so sure! He had studied every collection of photographs he could find, shot several hundred feet of film and spent uncounted hours in the darkroom learning to print. He had learned enough to land a few portrait assignments and to be his high school's yearbook photographer for two years. And so why not dream of working for the *Sentinel* . . . it could lead to a San Francisco paper and then maybe an agency that would send him all over the world. But, dreaming, he had been too vulnerable. It had not mattered that Beverly's was just one man's opinion.

After the interview, filled with the blind hurt of disappointment, he had joined Harrison Beebe and Bill West in a booth at the drugstore, and for half an hour had threatened to sell his camera. Beebe was sympathetic. But Bill West, a Modoc Indian, sat there without word or expression until Greg was finished. Then he shrugged and said, "Take the pictures he wants and try again." Good advice, but not in Middlefork.

It was a bustling lumber town, as sleepy as the Fourth of July. But tucked away on the Smith River, at the northwest edge of Six Rivers National Forest, it was still a small town where little ever happened. And so there was no time to assemble a new portfolio. If he was to try the *Sentinel* again and have any kind of chance, it meant finding two or three photographs that were nothing less than superb and finding them fast.

Over Cokes, the three had looked for ideas. But once past the obvious things like chasing fire engines and ambulances, which could involve too much waiting for something that might not even pan out, the suggestions had become preposterous. Bill offered to go to the Klamath Lake reservation, home for most of his nineteen years, and recruit relatives and friends for a fake Indian attack on Middlefork. Beebe thought of making huge footprints in the courthouse lawn, to go with a

3

sign that said BIGFOOT FOR SHERIFF. Finally giving in to the humor of it, Greg's idea was to photograph the town swimming pool and superimpose a shot of the sinking *Titanic*. It was good for a laugh.

Retrieving his pillow, Greg punched it and settled on his side to watch the dim rectangle of his window. He wanted to stop thinking about it. But . . . that Six Rivers country, the Siskiyou range . . . it was raw, rugged country . . . an emptiness that, in a sense, was no more familiar to man than the sea bottoms. Of course, men had mapped it from the air and watched it from fire-lookout towers, and it had been invaded by hunters. But that kind of thing meant only surface exploration. It was too big and wild to *know*.

That night, after the drugstore session, he had gone to bed wishing to be anywhere but in Middlefork. But there had to be *something* to photograph. In desperation, Greg finally went back over all that had been said . . . and struck an unexpected spark. Beebe's idea was utter nonsense, but something else came out of it, and he could not let go. At three in the morning, he had gotten Bill and Beebe out of their beds and confronted them with it.

"Why not try to photograph Bigfoot?"

Beebe was angry. "You're out of your gourd! If you want that job, you can't go chasing after something that *ain't!*" And Bill said quietly, "Look, some medicine man got a funny idea once . . . Beebe's right."

Barely above a whisper, Greg had said, "Then I'll go by myself, because you're wrong . . . both of you."

"You're kidding . . . aren't you?" Beebe watched him closely.

Apparently not needing to be told again, Bill had sighed. "Well, Beebe, how do you feel about a little camping trip?"

It was not that simple, of course. One did not just decide and go. An expedition, properly supplied and equipped for the wilderness, was an expensive proposition. Between them, they had some camping gear and a little money, but not nearly enough. What was needed was a sponsor. Greg tried the chamber of commerce, the big lumber mill, and some of the smaller merchants, but without success. Beaten, but not wanting to admit it, he had finally swallowed enough pride to go back to the *Sentinel* and ask Beverly. And to his surprise, the editor agreed to back them for two weeks in return for pictures and story. The expedition, success or failure, would make a good home-town feature.

"But I know why you're doing it," Beverly had said. "You must understand that my backing isn't intended as a commitment."

And Greg had asked, "What if I get a good shot of Bigfoot?"

The editor laughed. "Well . . . we'd certainly have to talk, wouldn't we?"

Greg's and Beebe's parents had to be asked, of course. Bill's were in Oregon, and he had only to get two weeks off from the lumber yard. But the parents saw nothing alarming in what, to them, was merely a camping trip. Bigfoot, after all, was just a legend.

5

With that, only detail remained . . . renting the camping gear, buying the food, acquiring two mules, and planning a search route. Even so, Greg had been too engrossed to back off and think. And now that the expedition was ready, he could not help being awed by the enormity of what had been set in motion.

He went to the window to watch the sky. The stars were bright, and he could almost see the first ridge rising to the east . . . and beyond it, the edges of emptiness. Somewhere out there, huddling in its own primeval dark, was Bigfoot. He was sure of it.

Indian legend, centuries old, told of Sasquatch. One had to consider superstition, he knew. Still, even among the first settlers, there was an awareness of something beyond the reach of lanterns. But it was in the last two decades or so, when the wilderness areas from California to British Columbia had shrunk so rapidly, that most of the evidence came to light . . . discoveries of footprints, possible sightings . . . and in remote logging camps, at night, bulldozers turned over and huge spools of cable tossed about. Anthropologists found more than could be explained by hoax. According to estimate, based on the number and spread of reports, there were at least a few hundred of the creatures and maybe as many as two thousand.

A dozen times Greg had tried to imagine finding Bigfoot. There were a few bad photographs, if legitimate, of a great hairy creature . . . the anthropologists were talking in terms of a cousin to the Himalayan *yeti* or Abominable Snowman. And somewhere he had heard a reference to a third group of perhaps similar creatures living high in the Andes. The size and depth of the footprints and measure of stride indicated that Sasquatch was an anthropoid of considerable size. Some adult males apparently attained a height of ten feet.

But beyond such descriptions, what was it? A kind of man that never made it across evolutionary distance? Was it intelligent or brutishly simple? And how would Sasquatch react to a more than accidental encounter with man?

The latter question was of considerable importance. Greg could not buy, borrow or rent a big telephoto lens in Middlefork. To get a good shot of Bigfoot, then, he would have to make every effort to get fairly close . . .

Greg pressed his face against the cool glass of the window wishing he had never heard of Bigfoot.

Mostly on impulse, he had committed friends and a man's money to an effort that, most likely, would be only a long walk, or *if* successful, might be dangerous. And it was too late to back out . . .

2.

The expedition was late in getting started. Greg had slept through the alarm and woke to Beebe's irritated rapping at his window. And Bill was late to arrive, his considerable patience somewhat tried by two long-eared, jug-headed characters named Pyramus and Thisbe. The mules had to be goaded and pulled most of the mile from Sheep Pen Flat, where they had been contentedly browsing in deep, dew-wet grass. Then, of course, there was the aggravating task of getting the packsaddles on and loaded. Bill was the only one who had ever seen it done. But seeing and doing were two different things. Though Bill pronounced them sufficient to survive the day, the canvas packs were not the neatest ever to decorate a mule. Then, just as they coaxed the mules into motion, the boys had to stop again.

Apple-cheeked, hair in curlers, and still in her dressing gown, Liz Anders came rushing out with a large paper bag and thrust it upon the nearest of them, which happened to be Beebe.

"A whole fried chicken," she said. "Apples and cookies."

"But Mom," Greg protested, "we're already packed!"

"Three strong boys can manage a grocery bag, I'm sure."

"But Missus Anders . . ." Beebe started, and then looked to Greg for help.

Greg tried to reason with her. "Mom, we're going to be too busy. And we don't need it. We really don't."

It probably would have been a losing argument had George Anders not come out then, on his way to work. He relieved Beebe of the bag, and said, "I know two lawyers and an overworked secretary who can put this to much better use."

"George . . ."

"Now Liz . . . I'm sure Stanley's mother didn't make him carry a lunch pail when he went looking for Livingstone! The boys have it all planned, and they're doing fine. Let them be." With a wave, George Anders sent them on their way.

Their starting place was in front of the *Sentinel* office, part of the plan being to photograph the start and advertise the paper's part in the expedition. To the packs were fastened signs that read: BIGFOOT EXPEDITION SPONSORED BY SIX RIVERS SENTINEL. The paper's photographer came out to take the first picture, so that they all could be in it. But Greg waved him aside and went across the street with his camera and tripod, and setting the self-timer device, ran back to pose with his friends. Then they proceeded eastward down Main Street, which was also U.S. Highway 199. What might be a hundred miles or more had begun . . .

Pyramus and Thisbe had resigned themselves to the fact of their labor and had settled down. But it was still slow going. Because of the late start, downtown Middlefork was busier than they had anticipated. They created one of the town's few traffic jams and drew a crowd. Except for the absence of banners and a brass band, it began to look like a celebration, and some young children even followed them out to the town limits. But there, the boys put asphalt behind and turned north into a beginning quiet.

"Well . . ." Beebe took a deep breath. "Here goes nothing."

Bill West remained silent, but his dark eyes fed on the land before them.

And Greg looked around as if he were in a troubled dream. Some of last night's anxieties still shadowed him, and it was hard to believe that the whole crazy thing had happened and was actually in motion.

At noon they stopped to eat a cold lunch and rest a little. Bill drove iron stakes into the ground and tethered the mules so that they could graze. Greg used the time to get a few shots.

"You got a funny eye," Beebe said, making a face. "It's big and glassy . . . and it goes click."

"Some of these pictures will be in the paper," Greg

told him, "so quit horsing around. It'd be better if you'd just forget that there's a camera being used."

"Didn't your dad want you to be a lawyer?" Beebe grumbled.

"Yes. We used to fight about it a lot. But now he sees it my way."

Beebe sighed. "That's unfortunate. Look what it let loose in the world."

"Relax!"

"But it makes me feel funny."

"Yeah." Bill tossed black hair away from his eyes and grinned. "But he has to have pictures because you're going to be famous."

"How so?"

"Harrison Beebe," Bill said, as if reading a headline, "the first man to be carried off and eaten by Sasquatch!"

"Sasquatch?" Beebe came up on one elbow.

"Bigfoot," Bill translated.

Beebe looked down his skinny six-foot-three frame and shook his head. "Like Chinese food. Two hours later, he'd be hungry again. Greg is a better candidate. More meat . . . if he doesn't scare the poor thing off with that big glass eye!"

Greg smiled. "All right. What do you say we get this thing back on the road?"

For most of the day they moved between the ridges, through meadows and stands of pine, firs and hardwoods. There were redwoods, too, but they were mere youngsters of a few centuries compared to the giants that once dominated here. This was land that had known the bite of saw and ax long before selective logging and reforestation came into practice. What grew there now was largely second growth . . . gifts of the wind.

With each mile, the boys felt more and more the impact of being committed to wilderness. They had long since passed the point where, if anything happened, they could turn around and reach home that day. And the sun was getting low.

Beverly had asked them to stay on the planned route, and in the event of trouble, stop and make a signal visible from the air or head for the nearest lookout tower, on the chance it might be manned . . . or send somebody back by mule . . . the choice depended on where they were and the nature of the trouble. And as an added precaution, a search would be mounted if they were more than three days late. But while working all that out in advance had been reassuring, it was one thing to study a map, and quite another to see the emptiness growing around them. They felt very small and alone.

It was not until evening that they passed into an untouched region of shadows and silence and made camp among ancient redwoods. The boys were not unfamiliar with that kind of forest. *Sequoia sempervirens* grew wherever the sea fogs reached, and one never had to travel far in northern California to see them. But being here was different than visiting one of the well-tailored

12

parks set aside for the touring public. The difference was that they were alone. There were no careful pathways and no sounds of other people. There was nothing here but the giants themselves, rising through silence and attended only by soft sprays of primeval fern . . . and the boys were subdued by it.

Some of the trees had been seedlings when Christ was born, and a few were much older. The feeling of antiquity was almost palpable . . . there was a sense of being surrounded by wordless intelligence. It was cathedral-like and like being in the depths of a strange kind of sea. Bill, Greg and Beebe had, in a way, left the world of man. They did not belong there, really . . .

Only when the giants retreated into the dark, beyond the fire, did the boys become more their usual selves. It helped, having a hot meal and settling back to enjoy a cheerful crackling fire. And maybe ten miles were behind them; it was easy to relax.

Greg had lived with the fact of the expedition long enough now to feel easier about it, and was content to reload his camera and hook up the flash gun on the chance it might be needed that night. But Bill and Beebe, though enjoying the trip, had returned to scoffing at the idea of Bigfoot.

Beebe finally turned to Greg. "It makes no sense. People have been living in this part of the state since the early 1800s."

"In small numbers," Greg replied. "And not so many even now."

"Compared to other places, sure," Beebe went on.

13

"But it stands to reason that if these things were running around out here, we would've seen them by now. Really seen them! Bill knows more about it than I do, but it seems to me there are animals that are pretty good at staying out of sight, and . . ."

"Fox, mountain lion," Bill offered. "Even hunters don't see them often."

"Yeah . . . I guess it's kind of rare to see one of those big cats, but we've seen them enough to know they're *real*. Those pictures of Bigfoot look like somebody in a gorilla suit. And the bulldozers getting turned over could be a logging crew having fun. The footprints are a joke because they're too easy to fake."

Greg put the camera and flash near his sleeping bag. "Sure, a lot of it has been faked . . . and I don't doubt that many of the reports were made by untrained observers who couldn't be sure of what they saw. But the investigations haven't always turned up that kind of answer. Yes, the prints are easy to make. The size aside, they look human, after all. But in some of the prints, there's been a subtle difference in bone structure . . . something a guy pulling a prank isn't likely to know. And as for seeing Bigfoot . . ."

"Yeah," Beebe interrupted, "if there are two thousand . . ."

"That's between here and southern Canada, for crying out loud!" Greg told him. "Listen, when I talked to Beverly, I asked him what he thought of Bigfoot, and he said he didn't know. But he told me a story, a true one . . . back at the turn of the century, a *stone-age*

14

man, sick and starving, came out of some pocket in the Sierras. He was found and taken to the University of California . . . I think . . . for care and study. When they taught him English, they learned he was the last of his tribe."

Beebe shrugged. "There are still stone agers in the world. The Australian Aborigine . . . and some in New Guinea, I think."

"But don't you see the point?" Greg asked him. "Fifty years before, that man's tribe managed to stay hidden in the middle of the Gold Rush! And the Rush brought *more* people into the Sierras than are probably living in the northern counties right now."

Beebe was quiet for a moment and then chuckled. "Bill, maybe we should've brought along a box of giant corn plasters for old Bigfoot!"

Greg laughed, but it was clear that he had not changed their minds. Not Beebe's at least, and it was not surprising. Maybe he had been shaped by his father's narrow world . . . a world that revolved around an automobile dealership, a world in which money was life's only objective. But whether it was his father's fault or not, Beebe was entirely too cautious and conservative to accept the possibility of Bigfoot easily.

But Bill . . . Greg wondered about him. The Modoc had turned from his people and the reservation when he was only thirteen or fourteen, and in spite of his age, managed to make his way. Between then and now, he had worked at a dozen jobs. And he had gone through most of high school. He was, in short, Beebe's opposite.

15

Too independent to be caught in a narrow world, his was wide and full of possibilities that had to be explored. And maybe, Greg decided, that was what was happening now . . . exploring the possibility of Bigfoot. Perhaps the idea had grown stronger with the story of that stone-age man. But Bill continued to watch the dancing shadows beyond the fire and didn't say what he was thinking.

3.

The second day was uneventful. They cooked breakfast, talking quietly and watching the first of the sun touch the top of one of the ancient trees. That patch of gold was over three hundred feet above the forest floor; it hardly belonged to the world they wandered. And when breakfast was done, after they had scrubbed tin plates and cooking utensils in the sand and icy water of the creek, the boys loaded the packs on Pyramus and Thisbe. The sun was still remote and lost to them when they moved on.

They watched the ground and the forest around them, alert for any sign of their quarry . . . sudden and furtive motion or places where the soft carpeting had been disturbed. It was Greg's belief that their best chance of finding traces of the creature was in following the canyon bottoms where water ran. Bigfoot, like any wild creature, had to drink.

But it was hard to remain alert. The silence of that forest was so profound and so devoid of indication that anything had ever been there that there were times when they might as well have been walking in their sleep. After a while, Beebe slipped into a state of unseeing and stayed there. Bill, too, seemed lost somewhere within himself, emerging only when their path led them through a slanting shaft of sunlight. Encountered in a shadowed region, those ladders of gold were startling in their warmth and brightness, and painfully beautiful.

While Greg understood what was happening, and indeed was not immune to it himself, he was angry by the time they stopped to eat.

"Man, I don't know what good you guys are! Sure, you came along even though you don't believe in the thing, and I appreciate that . . . but if you're going to get wiped out every time we hit a stretch of redwoods . . . well, I should've come by myself!" Saying it, Greg looked around and wondered if he could have come alone . . . and doubted it.

Bill quietly put a sandwich together and began eating. And Greg, making do with a couple of fruit bars, stretched out to contemplate a far fragment of sky. But Beebe had yet to even sit down. He watched Greg for a moment longer before finally giving in to what he felt. "Okay, so why don't I head for home?"

"Take it easy," Bill mumbled with a full mouth. "Sit down and eat. Long time until supper."

"Why? If there's no point in me being here, then . . ."

"Aw for crying out loud, Beebe!" Greg sat up. "It wasn't just you! Bill was doing it, too . . . and to tell the truth, so was I. I lost my temper and took it out on you guys, that's all. I'm sorry. Okay?"

Embarrassed now, Beebe slowly sat down. He said nothing until Bill thrust a sandwich in his direction. "Well . . . maybe if we talked more . . ."

Bill shook his head. "No. That's not the way you hunt for something . . . not when you can't see very far."

"What's the difference? Pyramus and Thisbe aren't exactly a couple of elves tiptoeing from mushroom to mushroom!"

With just enough impatience to sound condescending, Bill said, "Sure, Beebe, but it's an *animal* noise. And that's a lot different than human voices."

Clearly annoyed, Beebe threw the remainder of his sandwich away and sat there nodding. "Indians know just about everything, don't they."

"Yep," Bill agreed, with the faintest part of a smile in his eyes. "Especially Modocs."

"All right . . . lay off . . ." Beebe sputtered and began to grin. Then, indicating the forest around them, he said, "I guess we'll just have to get used to it."

And so they went on after a while, and if nothing else, they had blown off some of that growing pressure . . .

The night had come into its deepest quiet. Without wind, the trees were voiceless, and the owl that had mellowed the earlier hours was gone. Once as bright and loud as a celebration, the fire had now dimmed and was merely warm. The creek spoke across its stones, but that gentle sound became a part of silence, unless one thought to listen. The boys leaned on their elbows, quiet now and almost ready for sleep.

Stirring with some final spasm of restlessness, Beebe left the fire and rummaged through the stack of supplies. Greg sleepily watched him stand up and start to unwrap a candy bar, and then paid no more attention . . . not until Beebe stiffened, and with exaggerated slowness, came back to the fire.

"I saw something out there," he whispered.

"Huh?" Greg sat up.

"In a patch of moonlight . . . something moving . . ."

His fingers shaking with the suddenness of it, Greg picked up the camera and flash unit and, almost forgetting to remove the lens cover, went out to where Beebe had been.

The forest on that side of camp was a little more open, and so its floor was a patchwork of dark and moonlight. Greg stood there for several minutes waiting for something to happen. And tense with expectation, it was too easy to find in that multitude of black and silver night images, something to catch and tease the mind. Too easy to find part of a face with an eyeless hollow . . . and then an old man, mostly lost in darkness, sitting on a chair . . . and far out on the edge of it all, as if in a hidden garden, a girl in a long white gown.

20

Ghosts? He blinked his eyes and dismissed them. But the ending of one illusion allowed another to begin, and for a while, to be believed. Greg was too ready for such things, too primed . . . so much so that he almost yelled at the sight of those images suddenly beginning to move. Sweat bursting from his pores, he retreated a few stumbling steps before he realized what it was and stopped, feeling limp and foolish. Too high and too soft to be heard, the gentlest of night winds had stirred in the trees and made shadows come alive.

Greg took a deep breath, not knowing whether he was relieved or disappointed. But if there had ever been anything out there, it was gone now. He returned to the fire, cold and damp, and still shaking a little.

For a while, nothing was said. The three of them sat there peering into the dark beyond the fire. It was Beebe who finally broke the silence.

"But I *saw* something!"

"What?" Greg asked him. "Can you describe it?"

Beebe thought about it for a moment, and then shook his head in obvious aggravation. "No! Just an impression . . . you know what I mean? Look, it wasn't a bush, and it wasn't a tree. I *know* that much. But it was . . . well, *something!*"

"Maybe you only imagined it," Bill said.

"It's easy enough," Greg said. "The way those shadows move, it could've been an optical illusion . . . it sure had me going for a minute."

"But . . ." Beebe sat there with growing frustration, and then gave up. "I don't know. Maybe you're right."

21

"And maybe I'm not," Greg said. "Just because I jumped at shadows, that doesn't mean I was seeing the same thing you did. I think we ought to look for footprints in the morning."

"Why not right now?" Beebe stood up. "The flashlight ought to be enough.

"Too easy to mess things up with our own big feet," Bill muttered and ate the candy bar Beebe had forgotten.

Beebe sat down again. But then, as if itching with it, he asked, "Why don't we have a gun? I mean . . . suppose that *was* Bigfoot I saw, and he comes roaring right into camp? What do we do, get him with a can opener when he isn't looking?"

"We've been over all that."

"He wasn't with us that time," Bill reminded him. "Remember?"

"Oh . . . well, we decided we didn't need a rifle. From what we know, Bigfoot avoids contact with people. I'm not forgetting the business of turning bulldozers over. But whether that was curiosity, playfulness or resentment over the invasion of his territory, there's no record of Bigfoot attacking *people*. Another thing . . . not having a rifle might even be an advantage. The way hunters swarm into the mountains, shooting at anything that moves, it's possible Bigfoot knows about guns and is afraid of them. Unarmed, we might have a chance of getting closer with the camera."

"Okay," Beebe said. "But there's always a first time.

Like we find a Bigfoot that's *different!* It's not impossible . . ."

"No, it isn't." Greg let his breath out slowly. "And I guess we should have something worked out . . . some kind of defense."

"We already have something," Bill told them. "Wild animals don't like fire."

Greg nodded. "True, except our fire burns pretty low while we're asleep. I suppose we could gather extra wood and get up a few times during the night. But it seems to me we're tired enough when we make camp without adding that kind of routine."

"That's for sure!" Beebe agreed.

"We'll throw on some bigger chunks of wood before we turn in," Bill said. "But we need something to make it flare up fast if we have to."

Beebe held up a twig. "How about keeping a pile of small kindling on hand?"

"No." Greg frowned with the problem. "Even that stuff takes awhile to catch."

"Oil," Bill decided.

Puzzled, Greg looked at him. "What oil?"

"For waterproofing our boots."

"Hey, that's right!" Greg went to get it from their supplies. "This ought to do the job." Remembering that he would be grabbing for his camera in such an event, he gave the can of oil to Beebe to keep by his sleeping bag.

With that, they gradually settled back and began to

talk of other things. Sleep would be longer than usual in coming that night.

"What happened to that candy bar?" Beebe slapped his shirt pocket and peered around.

"I ate it," Bill confessed.

"Thanks!"

Bill shrugged. "Go get another one."

"No thanks!" Beebe crawled into his sleeping bag.

Greg laughed. "You sound as if you believe in Bigfoot?"

"Just for now," Beebe said.

"Why just for now?"

"Because it's too dark out there where the rest of the candy bars are, that's why! You crazy Indian, why didn't you get your own candy bar?"

"It was alone and unprotected."

"So what?" Beebe demanded to know.

"Indians ambush things."

Morning was slow in reaching that canyon and slower still in finding the forest floor. When bright sun burned across the high ridges, it was still dawn among the redwoods. The boys huddled together and fixed their breakfast. Not until the light was sufficient for a search did they move away from the fire and start looking for footprints.

They concentrated on the general area where Beebe thought he had seen something move. The boys established perhaps a hundred-foot circle around the spot and carefully worked their way across it, studying every

24

inch for any indication that the floor had been disturbed.

According to estimate, the larger specimens of Bigfoot weighed as much as a thousand pounds; plaster casts of his prints had produced measurements of fifteen inches or more in length and about six inches wide. But, unfortunately, it had not rained for a while, and neither had there been a fog for several days. Too, the natural replacement of foliage over the centuries had produced a soft but rather springy carpeting on the forest floor. Only a sharp-footed animal could have left obvious traces in it.

Beebe finally stopped short and got down on his knees. "Hey you guys, I think I found something!"

Bending close, Greg and Bill studied the spot he outlined with his finger. It was slightly darker than the space around it, as if the carpeting had been turned over, and there was a slight depression . . . or so it seemed. They could not find another one, even outside the circle, and so were not sure of what they had. The spot was too vague and too dim to tell them anything, and as such was not even worth a photograph. And yet it was undeniably different than all the ground around it . . .

"Don't know," Greg said, finally. "What do you think, Bill?"

"Beats me. I see it . . . but maybe after last night, I'm expecting to see something . . . you know?"

Greg frowned. "I'd hate to waste a day, staying

25

here for nothing. On the other hand, if this thing indicates some kind of a chance . . ."

"So what's a day," Beebe said. "I don't think it'd hurt us or the mules to take a break. We can make up the distance later."

"All right," Greg agreed. "If nothing more happens by tomorrow morning, we'll move on."

The boys did little that day. Greg took a few photographs, and Bill gave Pyramus and Thisbe a good wipedown while they fed on a ration of grain. Beebe read a book he had brought along. And wanting to be alert that night, they all grabbed some sleep late in the afternoon.

There was nothing they could point at and give a name, nothing tangible to say that the forest was not as it had been only minutes before. And yet it was strangely disquieting to watch the sun go down . . . to feel and almost hear the gathering dark. They built a fire, cooked supper, and with growing tension clung to the pinpoint of light they had made in that vast, drowning black. But if anything had come the night before, it did not come again. Not, at least, to be heard or seen . . .

4.

On the fourth day, shortly after sunrise, the expedition broke out of the redwoods and into Douglas fir country. It was a welcome but almost startling change to hear insects, to see birds flying. There were also jackrabbits and an occasional deer. The wind was no longer a song that was remote and lost in green, and they had the sky and sun now.

In no way were they any closer to civilization. Each step still took them deeper into wilderness. Indeed, by early afternoon they had crossed the remote North Fork of the Smith River. But however unpeopled and distant, they were back in their own kind of world.

It was an odd ghost that came to them in the evening. The boys had traveled an extra hour that day, to make up part of the distance lost the day before. And

27

there in a darkening valley . . . a trace of smoke and the smell of meat and beans.

"I don't get it." Beebe sniffed the air, puzzled. "Maybe we've been going the wrong way."

"No." Bill nodded at the last of a lemon sky behind them. "I've been watching our direction. It matches the map."

Greg squinted at the map. "Well . . . there *is* a lookout tower two or three miles to the south of us and another about four miles to the northeast . . . but I don't think we could smell somebody's supper that far."

"No, and the wind's wrong for it anyway," Bill said.

The boys moved on, curious but more concerned at the moment with finding a reasonably clear and level place to camp before the light failed them completely. After a few hundred yards, they came to a clearing that met the requirements. A creek wandered at its edge, and there by the water, they found a sandy place where they could build a fire and spread the sleeping bags. The mules could be put on long tethers and graze to their hearts' content. Because of a slight rise toward the center of the clearing, they did not see the cabin at first.

"Well," Greg said, "you guys want to go on, or what?"

"Too dark," Bill said. "But we better ask."

Leading Pyramus and Thisbe toward the cabin, the three got no farther than the rise before their presence was known. The door opened, and silhouetted against lantern light, a man peered out and waved at them to come closer.

When they were near enough to see, the boys found themselves being greeted by a small, hairy, dirty troll-like figure.

"Now if you fellers ain't a surprise." The man spoke with a kind of uncertainty, as if he had almost forgotten how to talk. "Nobody been here since I come. Eight years it be. Give them flop-ears some rope and come on in."

Greg thanked him and said, "We don't want to be a bother. We were looking for a place to camp for the night when we saw your cabin, and we thought we'd better ask your permission."

"That's real thoughty of you." The man gave a grin full of gaps. "I ain't got much place for sleepin', but I kin throw in some more beans and meat, and we can have ourse'fs a feed!"

"No, please . . ." Greg told him. "We thank you, but . . ."

"Ain't listenin'. You dig out your plates because I ain't got enough . . . but I sure got talkin' to do. Name's Morgan."

There seemed to be no polite way to refuse. Morgan was obviously starved for company and would not be put off. And so they tethered the mules, got their eating utensils out, and joined their strange host.

The squalid, ramshackle cabin smelled of man and greasy food. Its narrow, cluttered space told them as much about Morgan as did the man himself. Morgan was both trapper and recluse. Twice a year, he said, he made the trek to the town of Smith River to sell his furs. With the few dollars he made, Morgan pitched himself a "wall-eyed, ring-tailed drunk" to put his "innards" straight. Then, loading up with flour, beans, molasses and shells for his shotgun . . . as much as he could carry on his back . . . he headed for home again, having had enough of bad whiskey and people for a while. With the shotgun, Morgan rounded out his diet with deer, bear and rabbit, and he grew a few onions and potatoes in the clearing.

He never said why he removed himself so thoroughly from his own kind. Smith River was near the coast north of Middlefork and only ten miles away if one figured in a straight line. Allowing for the wanderings of canyons, however, the distance was probably close to thirty miles each way. And the measure of his exile became even more apparent when it was considered that, while of indeterminate age, Morgan was by no means a young man.

He was, in fact, quite brutally alone, and the scars of his choice were on him. Clearly, the man had come to madness. His eyes were bright with it, and his thoughts erratic. But while the boys felt uncomfortable in his presence, Morgan seemed harmless enough.

The trapper cleared space for them at the rough-cut table and filled their plates from a pot that, blackened and encrusted, showed the traces of too many other meals. The food itself, like the man and his shelter, seemed full of smoke and grease. Greg's stomach rebelled at every bite, and it was no easier for Beebe and Bill. But Morgan slumped and elbowed his way through the meal with loud and grinning gusto and expected the same of them.

It had to be endured. To reject the man's hospitality and push the food away was unthinkable; he had to carry his supplies too many miles. But as soon as the last bite was suffered, Greg went outside to their own supplies and came back with two large cans of sliced pineapple. It was a friendly gesture, of course, but it was also a quick way of forgetting a bad taste.

The old man brightened like a child at a birthday party, and obviously starved for such things, attacked the fruit in a near frenzy. Slowing down only to breathe, he consumed an entire can. With that, he pushed back from the table, sucked his teeth for a few minutes, and then looked at them as if weighing something in his mind.

"Well now . . . and what're you fellers up to? You golygists or somethin'?"

"*Golygists?*" Beebe raised his eyebrows.

"I think he means geologists," Greg said. "No sir, nothing like that. We're on a photographic expedition . . . you know, to take pictures."

Morgan stared at them. "You don't say. Pictures . . . I seen a calendar once . . . had a picture of a pretty lake and some mountains . . . snow up high . . . and you could see them mountains in the water. Pictures like that?"

"No," Greg told him. "Actually, we're looking for . . ."

"You sure didn't come all the way from Middlefork to take a picture of an ol' hunk of trap bait like me!" Morgan laughed, and they laughed with him.

Greg shook his head and said, "No, we're looking for Bigfoot."

The good humor, the whole mood of what had passed between them, shifted and was lost as quickly as spilled mercury. Morgan looked at them as if his hearing had been faulty. Both his eyes and voice were strange when he asked, "Bigfoot?"

"Yes, sir," Greg replied. "Bigfoot. Sasquatch. Maybe you haven't heard. It's a large, manlike . . ."

Slowly, almost casually, Morgan stood up, took his long, double-barrel twelve-gauge shotgun from the wall, and quietly sat down again. Resting the gun on his knee, he pointed it straight at them. The boys were too shocked to do anything but sit there and gape at the man.

Morgan blinked and slowly shook his head. "I can't have you fellers comin' through here and gettin' Bigfoot all stirred up . . . you oughta know better'n that! I gotta live with that creeter . . . and so far, me and Bigfoot gits along jes' fine. He don't bother me, and I don't bother him . . . and I mean for it to stay that way."

"You don't understand," Bill told him. "Nobody knows for sure that Bigfoot really exists. But even if he does, we sure didn't come out here to throw rocks or scare him or anything like that . . ."

"Well, I'll tell you fellers . . . he's out here all right . . . and you ain't goin' . . ."

"Have you *seen* Bigfoot?" Greg interrupted.

"Could make powder of a man's bones, and . . . and . . ."

"Wait." Greg tried again. "Have you actually seen him?"

"Why he could make kindlin' wood of this shack with one blow of his hand!" Morgan was raving now, and his eyes seemed out of focus. "And I built it strong . . . I sure did . . . it don't look like much, but you betcher life it's strong."

"He's flipped but good!" Beebe muttered.

"Maybe we can grab the gun . . . don't think he's seeing us," Greg whispered back.

"No!" Bill warned. "Don't underestimate him. He'll use it . . ."

"Got no right," Morgan mumbled. "Messin' around . . . ain't goin' to do it no more. Come mornin' . . ."

"What happens in the morning?" Beebe demanded.

"Ain't goin' to change what I got!" The old man spoke as if he were alone. "Ain't goin' to move again . . . even if I got to bury you . . ."

Morgan said nothing more. Nothing intelligible at least. He just sat there now with eyes that, like a snake's, did not blink. Whether he saw them or wandered instead in some twisted labyrinth of his mind, the boys could not know with any certainty. The only thing steady and calm about him were his hands, and they continued to hold the shotgun pointed with careful aim.

33

A little pressure on the trigger would blast the three of them right through the wall.

"What do you suppose he's seen?" Beebe kept his voice down.

"Don't know," Bill answered. "Something's had him scared . . . real scared . . ."

"Maybe Bigfoot . . ." Greg said.

Beebe flinched. "Don't even mention the name! So what now?"

"Wait," Bill told them. "Wait and watch for some kind of chance . . ."

Wait and watch . . . it was all they could do. Evening had become night, and now night had turned into nightmare.

5.

There were times, during the night, when Morgan uttered unheard words at them under his breath and times when some kind of electricity gathered and discharged along his muscles to make him jump as if jerked by a string. But those stirrings were only momentary, and not once, in all of that night, did he relax his vigil.

Only when the sky held a beginning gray, did the man show signs of change. Seeming to come from far away, Morgan sighed deeply, slumped a little, and began to blink his eyes more regularly. Greg watched it happen, wondering if the end of night, and any fears it might have held, could be making the difference. But there was no way of knowing if he had returned to a more relaxed state of mind or was merely bending under the weight of fatigue.

The best that could be said was that Morgan, in

some way, was closer to the surface . . . too close for the boys to whisper among themselves without risk of triggering some violent response in the man. Too, Morgan would be deciding what to do with them, if indeed the difference in him was not a sign that a decision *had* been made. For whatever time was left, then, they could only continue to watch and wait. And it was a brutal test . . . muscles demanded to move, eyes wanted to close, and after that many hours it was difficult to keep the mind from drifting into some uncaring place. Fortunately, Bill was the exception. Somehow more able to endure such pressures and like some curious bird of prey, he had not once taken his eyes off Morgan.

That sudden difference in Morgan retreated into time until it, too, became a seemingly unending sameness. It was as if one statue had been traded for another. Dawn grew old and died in a rim of fire, and the sun had begun to climb past the ridges and trees. What was the old man waiting for? Greg could not help wondering if Morgan, lost somewhere in madness, had yet to realize the fact of morning.

But then the sun rose high enough to strike the cabin wall. Its brightness found chinks between the logs and sent thin lines of yellow light through smoky darkness to touch the floor. Here were time and morning made obvious. The boys visibly tensed and no longer questioned Morgan's waiting. Marked by this brilliant contrast, time very clearly had to be running short.

After a few minutes, Beebe could not take it any more. "Look Morgan, I don't know what you're planning, but if we aren't back in Middlefork by a certain time, there'll be a lot of men searching for us. And they'll know where to look. They happen to have a map with our route drawn on it, and your cabin sits right on that route. Do you understand? You can even kill us and bury us a mile deep, and it won't do you a bit of good. When they don't find us anywhere else on that route, they'll come here . . . you can count on it!"

Morgan made no response and did not show any signs of caring. He just sat there and held the gun on them as before.

Greg tried another approach. "If you know about Bigfoot, then you know he tries to stay out of sight of people. You know we don't have much chance of finding him, especially in the daytime. And if you let us go, we'd be ten miles away by dark . . . too far to cause you trouble."

Morgan reacted to it, and sounding vaguely nervous, growled, "I ain't takin' no chances like that! I told you, me and Bigfoot gets along fine. And it's goin' to stay that way."

"You crazy old . . ." Beebe was halfway to his feet.

"Cool it." Bill stopped him. "Take it easy."

Morgan, who had raised the shotgun a few inches, grinned and lowered it again. "Bill's smart," he said. "Real smart . . ."

Motionless silence . . . they were falling into it again. It seemed to Greg that Morgan had two choices. Murder, of course. Or simply ending the expedition by killing the mules, smashing the camera, or destroying their supplies. But what in God's name was the man waiting for? Greg knew that the waiting could be nothing more than a quirk of Morgan's mind. But if not that, then time was somehow important . . . this, combined with the way Morgan had dismissed Beebe's threats and responded only to mention of Bigfoot, gave Greg an idea that was both tantalizing and eerie. Maybe Bigfoot lived in the land just ahead . . . maybe one of the creatures or even a family frequented Morgan's part of the forest at a certain time of day.

"Morgan . . ." Greg was hesitant, trying not to aggravate the old man. "I can't help asking . . . do you see Bigfoot often? I mean, do you have one coming to the edge of the clearing every day? Is that why we're waiting?"

Something moved behind Morgan's eyes, and his mouth twitched as if killing a word. And that was all. But in the silence that followed, Greg wondered if he had not hit on the truth . . .

It was more than an hour before something new was added to that scene. Greg would not have seen it had it not been for Bill's sudden interest . . . the Modoc had detected motion above them, where the wall met the slanting underside of the roof. It must have climbed the corner logs outside and then moved along one of the logs to where a seam widened, but inside the cabin now and inching along a rafter was a small and pretty snake.

Bill pointed at the rafter. "You have a visitor."

Morgan allowed himself a quick look, and shrugged. "Jes' a leetle ol' king snake. Good to have around." Bill apparently saw some kind of glimmer and so continued the conversation.

"I've heard they go after rattlesnakes."

"That's right, boy. Never kill a king snake."

"No," Bill agreed. "Be like killing a friend. But I guess when you find one, it might mean there's a rattlesnake around . . ."

Beebe took the cue and nervously looked about. "Hey, does that mean there might be a rattlesnake in here?"

"There's enough holes in this place," Greg said. "Could have come in during the night without us knowing it!"

Morgan coughed with what might have passed for a laugh. "No point in gittin' all spooked up. Now if this leetle king snake'd been here yesterday and was still hangin' around . . ." He hesitated, and then, as if something had come to haunt him, a tight little trembling touched him and made it hard for him to speak. "Well . . . I wouldn't be sittin' here! I don't mind sayin', I hate rattlers more'n anythin'!"

The opportunity this held could not have been more obvious, and the three of them were quite aware of it. But they wondered if it would work . . .

Bill gave Beebe an almost imperceptible nod.

"But . . ." Beebe put a lot of uncertainty in his voice. "But . . . I think it *was* here yesterday . . ."

39

"What're you jawin' about boy?" Morgan's eyes narrowed.

"The king snake . . . I saw something not far from the door when we came in yesterday. By the wall outside. I think it was a snake . . ."

"No you didn't."

"Maybe you're right." Beebe shrugged. "Must've been something else."

Morgan seemed to let it go. He did not move, and the silence returned. The old trapper went on watching them . . . waiting for something or planning.

Perhaps, in his madness and solitude, Morgan was a man of many fears. Whatever the case, after ten or fifteen minutes it became apparent that something was working on him. He began to fidget and kept shifting the position of his legs, as if his ankles bothered him. Finally he looked up to locate the king snake again.

They *had* planted a seed, then, and it was growing and working on him. It gathered in Morgan like an itch, and the boys bided their time, waiting as they would for a man who, sooner or later, would have to scratch.

It took several minutes more, but Morgan jerked in his seat and stood up. Looking at Beebe, he said, "You seen that king snake yesterday."

"Maybe. I'm not sure," Beebe told him.

"Well, mebbe I oughta look around . . . but you boys don't try nuthin'! I still got m'gun!"

Cautious, not taking his eyes off them for more than seconds at a time, Morgan began prowling around

40

in the cabin's clutter. He looked under his cot and behind boxes . . . the sacks of potatoes and onions were suspect, and he was careful of the pile of cured furs, prodding it with his gun barrel. It was the first time that the gun had been turned away from them, and Beebe tensed with it. But a look from Bill stopped him . . . it was too far to jump.

There were only two places left, then. A washtub that was on the floor upside down . . . apparently Morgan sat on it far more than in it . . . and the stack of wood by the hearth. Morgan went to the wood, first, with a visible increase of tension. It was a likely place; the ashes still gave off warmth, which would attract a snake at night, and the firewood offered cover.

It was an awkward moment for the trapper. Still keeping an eye and ear out for his captives, Morgan also had to watch the logs as he moved them one by one. Sweat dripped from his face. If there was to be a time to catch him off guard, it had to be now, but still Bill held them back, warning them with his eyes. Morgan was down to the last eight or ten pieces of wood, and there weren't many spaces left where a snake might be found.

But he had moved only two more logs when Bill shouted, *"Look out!"*

The old man jumped back a step, swung the gun around, and still obeying nothing more than fearful reflex, blasted what was left of the woodpile.

"Now!" Bill snapped at them. Beebe, as if stunned by the explosion of the shotgun, could only sit there.

But Greg was up in an instant, and the two of them leaped for Morgan before he could swing around and use the other barrel. The impact of their bodies caught him hard, but for all his years, Morgan was a tough and wiry man. Somehow he stayed on his feet and fought to keep the gun. And in that close, intense struggle, it went off again . . .

6.

When the smoke cleared, the boys looked anxiously at each other and at Morgan. The old man had gone limp with the firing of the second barrel. But while the boys had felt the heat and concussion of it, it was the roof that took the charge . . . they saw the sky through a round and ragged hole. As for Morgan, it was a simple matter of being unarmed and no match for the two young men holding him.

Looking down at Beebe, Bill asked, "What happened to you?"

"I . . . it was so fast," Beebe stammered. "I'm sorry."

"Oh, I thought maybe you'd been hit . . . some of that first shot bounced off the fireplace. Okay, so let's get things moving."

"What're we going to do with Morgan?" Greg wanted to know.

Studying the old man's eyes, Bill said, "Guess we'll have to take him along."

Beebe took a deep breath and stood up. "Why not leave him?"

"He might come after us," Bill told him.

Greg agreed. "But we could take his gun instead."

"No," Beebe objected. "We can't do that."

Greg was surprised. "Why not?"

"He needs it for meat. I don't see any point in causing the old screwball harm." Pointing at a cluttered shelf and a half-hidden box of ammunition, he said, "Why don't we take the shells with us, and leave the box where he could find it later."

"Beebe," Greg said with some impatience, "look around and tell me you can be sure that he couldn't dig up some more shells. I think he'd be drawing a bead on us before we got half a mile."

Bill quietly put one shell in the gun. "We're taking Morgan with us for half a day. Then, I'll take this shell out, give Morgan the gun and send him home. By the time he gets back here and can load it again, it'll be getting dark. He'll be tired, and we'll be a whole day from here."

Greg nodded. "It should work. Let's go."

The sun was halfway to noon when they finished watering the mules at the creek and were on their way again. They had lost a few hours that morning, and they were feeling the lack of sleep. And so ten miles, for that day, was probably out of the question, but no mention of the fact was made in Morgan's presence. They put him in front where he could be watched, and left the clearing to do the best they could with what remained of the day.

Morgan was silent and balky. Frequently, he had to be prodded with the shotgun and reminded that it was loaded. But it was a losing battle. The old man knew very well that he was not in danger of being shot. It was wanting his gun back and being outnumbered that kept him from breaking away or trying to regain the advantage. However, Morgan continued his delaying tactics and cost the boys in time and patience until Bill thought to put a rope around him and tie the other end to Thisbe. Whenever Morgan started dragging his heels and making a fuss, Thisbe tried to get away from him by going faster. The trapper gave up after the second time he lost his footing and went up the trail on his backside. The boys no longer had to pay him much heed.

But something began to change at about one o'clock. Morgan started laughing, and it was not the hysterical shrieking of a mad man. It was ordinary laughter, and somehow that made it more disturbing.

"Can you figure it?" Greg asked Beebe.

"No, but I wish he'd stop! It's making me as loony as he is!"

The only clue they had was in the interest Morgan paid to the country ahead of them . . . the farther they moved into it, the harder he laughed. But for all

45

they could see, the land ahead was like the land behind them; there was nothing unusual about it, and so they were forced to conclude that it was something in the man's mind rather than anything real.

Still, there was no way of shutting it out, and it began to eat at their nerves.

"You don't suppose he's got something planned," Beebe muttered to Greg.

"What could he do and with what?"

"I don't know." Beebe shook his head. "But I sure get the feeling he knows something we don't know, and that we're walking right into it . . . like a whole Bigfoot colony."

Greg grinned. "No, that's impossible."

"Oh yeah? Why?"

"Because they'd all be standing on each other's feet."

Beebe groaned. "I'd laugh, except I'm afraid of what I might sound like!"

At two o'clock, Bill called a halt and said it was time to send Morgan back. He took the shell out of the shotgun and gave the gun to the old man.

"I'm sorry we had to do this to you," Greg told him. "But you didn't give us much choice."

Morgan turned to go, but first he looked at the land ahead and then squinted at the sun. Seeming to have confirmed some measure in his mind, he smiled in a way that had their scalps crawling. "You fellers better be sorry for yourse'fs!"

With that, he left them and headed homeward,

laughing . . . and he was still laughing when they could no longer see him.

"His mind's gone, that's all," Greg said, but he could not dismiss the sound or forget it. And neither could the others . . .

7.

Inside another hour, the terrain ahead of them changed abruptly. It split into two ridges of harsh earth and stone, where scrubby and tenacious little pines were the only surviving green. Though no blackened traces of it remained, this sudden scar on the land was perhaps the result of some ancient holocaust.

Pyramus and Thisbe had to be considered. Too, Greg wanted to get down to water again, where there would be a better chance of finding signs of Bigfoot. And so they pushed misgivings aside and headed downward, between the two ridges.

The going was slow and difficult. There was a ghost of a path to follow, made by deer and other animals, but it was narrow and precipitous and too often covered with loose rock. The mules did not like it; footing was bad and downward progress was marked by small avalanches of stone that clattered away into the silence

48

of the canyon below. And it was hot . . . the afternoon sun burned across that rocky slope and the heat rose heavy and dry and was thick with their dust. It was almost four o'clock when they reached the bottom and slipped once more into the shadows of deep redwoods. There, they stopped to drink and wash the dust off their faces and to rest for a few minutes. It was a sharp and pleasant contrast, trading harsh stone glare for cool and shaded green. And the redwoods were beautiful in their awesome way. But Beebe watched the darkness they made on the earth and was restless.

"Look," he said, "for *real,* what was Morgan laughing at? We've got to know."

"Why don't you go back and ask him?" Greg replied.

"Don't get on me, Greg! I think it's important."

"The man's *crazy,*" Bill reminded him.

"Sure," Beebe said. "I'm not forgetting that. But he's also a trapper and probably knows this country as well as he knows the inside of his cabin. And I think we better start asking questions . . . whether it's real or not, this Bigfoot thing scares him . . . scared him enough to have him stay up all night to keep a gun on us and, I think, scared him enough to shoot us. Okay, so we get lucky and take the gun away and march him for a while before turning him loose. Why, all of a sudden, does he think it's funny? Just because he's crazy? Man, I don't think we ought to depend on that!"

"Let's get moving," Greg said. "We ought to do two or three more miles before we quit."

And so they moved deeper into the redwoods, following the small stream.

"What are the possibilities?" Beebe continued. "He was watching the way we were going . . . is there some way this area can be dangerous to us? You know, like quicksand or falling off of cliffs, rabid animals. I was joking before, but when you get right down to it, is there any reason why there couldn't be a Bigfoot colony, a whole bunch of them all in one place?"

Greg was quiet for a while, and then replied, "Except for that rocky stretch, the country seems no different than what we've already seen . . . if there was anything unusual about it, I think the map would show it. And what can I say about Bigfoot? Footprints have indicated family units, but I don't think anyone's found evidence of colonies. I don't know, Beebe . . . Morgan's laughing bothered me, too, but I think we let it get to us more than we should. I know he was interested in the direction we were traveling, but . . . well, I don't think he could possibly know where we were going."

"You're wrong about that," Bill said.

"Aw come on, now!" Greg protested.

"The man's a trapper and hunter, and he's had a long time to learn this country. He knew the direction we were taking, and he also knew that we'd have to go where our mules could go. And because we're looking for Bigfoot, he knew we'd head for water. He knew that we were tired, but that we still wanted to make up for the time lost this morning, and so he knew we'd take what looks like the easiest way. You better

50

believe that man knows exactly where we are right now!"

Greg shrugged it off. "Okay, so what difference does it make? You said yourself it wasn't likely he would go all the way home and then come after us again. So why not forget it?"

"Maybe we should," Bill said, "but one thing bothers me. Suppose he didn't have to go home to load his gun. I didn't think of it before, but trappers sometimes leave caches of supplies here and there when they have long traplines to work. Suppose he was only a mile or two away from a cache and suppose it included shotgun shells . . . well, that'd be a good reason for laughing. I think we better stop worrying about Bigfoot and what kind of country we're in and keep an eye out for old brother Morgan."

The canyon came to an abrupt end. The source of the creek was a spring, and rising above it was a vertical bluff of moss and fern-covered stone. To go on, they would have to climb to the right or to the left, and the canyon walls were steep and heavily timbered.

The hour considered, it seemed best to stay where they were. But Greg hesitated. "If Morgan knows as much as you say," he said to Bill, "then it just might be that he expects us to stop here."

"Now you're using your head," Bill agreed. "Let's climb. It looks a little easier to the left."

"Should we?" Beebe asked. "Wouldn't he expect that, too?"

"Yes, but I don't think he expects us to leave here

51

until tomorrow. Anyway, when we get out of here, maybe we can do something about covering our tracks, and it'd be smart if we didn't have a fire tonight. Come on, we're wasting time."

It was a difficult few hundred feet up through the trees. Pyramus and Thisbe would not have been able to make it were it not for soft earth in which to plant their hoofs. As it was, with their heavy packs working against them, they seemed in danger at times of tipping over backward. Twice, Thisbe's answer to it was to brace her rump against a tree and sigh miserably until coaxed into moving again. It would have been funny had they not needed to be elsewhere when darkness came.

When they emerged from the trees, they were only halfway to the ridge and entering another scarred and jumbled world of stone. But if the other place bore the scar of an old fire, that was not true here. It appeared as if the earth had collapsed and fallen away to expose its bones in a kind of frozen, motionless avalanche.

The boys stopped for a few minutes to study the way ahead. On both sides of this deep scar were low but sharp-rising cliffs. Any thought of climbing them was discarded; the mules could not make it. The only alternative, besides retreating downward and taking what seemed a much longer way around to the ridge, was to go through the rocks. And there did appear to be a path . . . a twisting, tortuous route that wandered between huge slabs and boulders, some of which were as big as a house.

Bill traced it with his eyes but then frowned. "It's going to be dark before we get through there. I don't like the look of it."

"We've got the light," Greg pointed out.

"Yeah, but don't you see the way that path goes? Once we're in there, we won't be able to turn the mules around."

"Why should we?" Beebe asked.

"If the mules get to a place that's too narrow for the packs," Bill replied, "it means unloading and not much room to do it."

Greg nodded. "You got a point, but we can't stay here. There's no way around the rocks, and I don't think we want to go back down to where we were."

"Okay." Bill shrugged. "Let's give it a try."

It was a strange transition, moving out of forest and into that jumbled maze of stone. The sun had gone behind some distant ridge, giving them a glowing kind of twilight. The soft earth had turned hard and the stone masses threw the heat of the day back at them. In that evening light there were no earth colors, only blues and blue grays. It was not unpleasant, just strange.

Within the first few yards, it became obvious that Bill had been right. There would be no turning the mules around and going back. And very quickly, they were reminded of the gamble by the sound of canvas rubbing across stone . . .

Greg grimaced. "That's close!"

Only a minute or two later, it happened again, and all they could do was keep the mules from stopping. But thus far, at least, the spaces between the boulders were still less restricted than they had seemed from below. Unless the nature of the path changed suddenly, it did not appear that the packs would cause any real trouble.

The farther they went into that stony labyrinth, the more they became aware of an odd, musky odor, and the dry rasping sounds of what seemed to be insects . . . locusts, perhaps. Bill was bothered by it; he kept slowing down, as if trying to remember something.

"Next wide space we reach," he said, "let's get the light out. Getting too dark to see."

Hearing the tightness in Bill's voice, Greg turned and asked, "What's the matter?"

"I don't know. Those bugs . . . they don't act right!"

"How do you mean?" Greg waited for him to catch up.

"Bugs that make noise . . . like a cricket . . . when you get close to them, they stop singing. Right?"

"Yeah," Greg said, "that's true."

"Okay, so this noise we're hearing *starts* when we get close. And another thing, the farther we go, the louder it gets. And it isn't just in front of us or to the sides any more . . . it's in back of us, too. Whatever it is, we're running into more and more of them. I don't like it. And I don't think we'd better wait. Get the light out *now*."

"All right . . . it's in Thisbe's pack. Beebe?"

"Yeah, I heard. Should've done it down below."

"No problem. Just loosen the flap on the right side and reach in. I put it where we could get at it."

"Huh? Oh, okay," Beebe said. "Boy, one of these things is beginning to buzz right in my ear . . . can you move up a few feet? Too narrow back here."

Bill pulled Pyramus forward, and as he did, something jumped or fell from an overhanging boulder, landing where Beebe had been an instant before. Thisbe surged forward with a squeal, almost running him down.

Beebe did not wait to find the flashlight, but took a wooden match from his pocket, struck it on stone and eased around Thisbe to have a look.

"No!" Bill suddenly yelled. "Don't go back there! I know what it is, now!"

8.

On the edge of a match's dim glow, evil shrank against stone and coiled in a way that was as fluid as smoke. Beebe stopped short in sudden recognition and slowly backed away.

"Beebe!" Bill warned him again. "It's a rattlesnake!"

"You don't have to tell me!" Beebe croaked. "I see it!"

"Oh my Lord . . ." Greg said. "All around us . . ."

Bill nodded grimly. "A whole colony of rattlesnakes. Maybe hundreds of them . . . well, now we know. Now we *really* know!"

"You mean Morgan?"

"What else! The way just the idea of a snake got to him. I'll bet he was here and made the same mistake we've made. Beebe, *where's* that light?"

Hearing no answer, they turned to look at him. And

it took a moment to realize how rigid he was . . . frozen there and staring at the ground at his feet.

"You all right, Beebe?" Greg started to go back, but Bill stopped him.

"That snake might've moved," he whispered. "Let me . . ."

Bill worked his way past Pyramus, moving only slow inches at a time. Reaching the interval between the mules, he stopped, and then almost imperceptibly bent down for a closer look at the spaces around Beebe's feet. After a very long minute, he straightened up and, twice, slapped Beebe's face hard.

"Hey . . ." Beebe collapsed into motion, staggering back out of reach.

Grabbing him before he could go too far, Bill slapped him again. "Get ahold of yourself! You hear me?"

"I . . . I'm . . ."

"You're scared! So am I! Now, go get the light out. *Move!*"

Beebe lurched woodenly to Thisbe's pack. He could not make his fingers work, and he was nearly sobbing when, somehow, the flap finally came loose.

Bill took the light from him and swept its brilliant beam around them. No matter where he swung the light, there was at least one snake, and in some places there were Medusa-like clusters of them. But as much as could be determined, the closest snake to them was maybe twenty feet away. They were reasonably safe for the moment.

Bill returned his attention to Beebe. "Knowing where they are helps a lot, doesn't it?"

Still shaking, but obviously pulling himself together, Beebe nodded. "I'm all right."

"Good. So let's . . ."

"Hold it a second." Greg interrupted. "Put the light on that nearest bunch of snakes. We ought to have a picture."

"*Now?*" Beebe could not believe it.

Bill moved the light around and found them. "Make it fast."

Greg unsnapped the case and removed the lens cap. Focusing on the snakes, he said, "Need a meter reading . . . okay . . . fifteenth of a second at f1.4 Ought to have the tripod, but maybe I can . . ."

"Quit gabbing about it and shoot!" Bill complained.

"Hold the light still . . . now . . ." He tripped the shutter. "Got it. So what now? We can't stay here, and we can't go back . . . they're behind us, anyway."

"We've got to keep going," Bill told him. "But it'd be better if we tied the mules together and the three of us stayed in front with the light. Beebe, you lead the mules, Greg works the light . . . and I'd better get the shovel."

"Wait!" Beebe protested. "You saw what happened when that snake jumped down on the path. Thisbe almost ran over me! How about letting the mules go ahead of us?"

"No, we've got to protect them and the supplies," Bill said.

58

"But, man . . ." Beebe looked back at the overhang and could not buy the idea. Neither could Greg.

"Take it easy. That snake didn't jump. When we stopped, it got so scared it *fell* off! And be glad we've got mules. Thisbe was just staying clear. Horses would've stampeded by now. No, what we do is take it slow and keep an eye on the path and off to the sides. And if we have to stop, we stay away from the overhangs. Okay?"

"I don't think it's going to be as easy as all that," Beebe muttered.

"Didn't say it was. But it's all we can do."

They tied Pyramus and Thisbe together, and with some difficulty, managed to get the collapsible camp shovel out of the pack without unloading everything.

Taking one more look at the arrangement, Bill nodded. "Let's go. And keep your eyes sharp. Under the light, they're going to be about the same color as the rocks. Another thing . . . they don't always rattle, so don't just watch where you hear them."

Bill went first, with Greg right behind him and to one side shining the light on the path ahead.

"I don't understand," Greg almost whispered.

"Snakes can't take direct sunlight," Bill explained. "But they like the warmth, so they come out at night and sit on the rocks. There's some big nests here . . . that's what we smell. But some of the snakes come down from the forest. Wait . . . shine it more to the left."

The light settled on silent and motionless coils. Its

59

flat, triangular head slightly raised, the snake watched them with unblinking eyes. Bill approached it cautiously, and only then did its rattles begin to sound.

"Take it easy," Beebe warned.

"Done it before," Bill assured them. When he was close enough to reach, the Modoc brought the shovel down with a short, hard thrust that cut the snake in two just a few inches behind its head. Since the dead snake was writhing around and still dangerous, Bill scooped it up on the shovel and gave it a fling.

"One down, ninety-nine thousand to go," Beebe said, a tremor in his voice.

They went on then, and Bill took to banging the shovel on the rocks, hoping to drive away in advance other snakes that might be waiting on the path. He knew snakes were deaf, but they could feel vibrations. And in that bright light it would be easy to see the sharp, warning swings of the shovel. But if Bill was clearing the path, he was also exciting the other snakes around them into a greater din.

It was difficult to move slowly and not give in to the strong impulse to run. That scene was too much like one of Dante's visions of Hell. The hissing, writhing serpents were all around them. Convulsed with fright and fury, they fell back in waves and tangles like sea grass caught in a changing and waterless tide. But there was no comfort in that retreat . . .

Time and time again, Bill had to stop their agonized progress and kill a snake on the path in front of them. Some were small, and a few were maybe five feet long and nearly as big around as a man's arm. But all were equally venomous and equally unnerving to encounter. Not counting the one that had almost fallen on Beebe, there had been six, and they had come in such rapid succession that Greg, feeling his own nerves stretching too tight, became concerned for Bill and called a halt.

"You all right? Want to rest for a few minutes?"

Bill turned, sweat dripping from his face; as if full of fever, his eyes seemed too bright. "No, keep going," he insisted. "I'm okay . . . doesn't bother me."

Greg could only continue sweeping with the light and trust that Bill was the best judge of himself. And maybe he *was* all right. But somewhere there had to be a limit, and he came to it only a few minutes later. Overwhelmed or simply running out of luck, Bill did not see the seventh snake.

A sudden sparking of motion caught Greg's eyes, but it was too quick to grasp. He did not really see it except as an afterimage in his mind. Bill was raising the shovel shoulder-high when that slender shadow flicked outward from stone. Jaws opened, its curving fangs flashing in the light, the snake struck Bill in the side . . . struck and hung there, twisting and coiling against itself. Bill dropped the shovel and looked down at himself . . . and yet, in some way, he did not seem to understand.

Breaking out of whatever ice it was that held him, Greg threw himself forward. With one move, he grabbed the snake, yanked it loose and threw it far from the

61

path. Strangely white, Bill looked at him for a long time, then sat down . . .

Beebe stared and tried to speak. But it caught in his throat and he turned away, trying not to be sick. Greg hovered over the Modoc, fighting for a hold on himself. His mind spun with it, and he could only drop to his knees helplessly. "Bill . . . what do we do?"

Doubled over and silent, his breath coming too fast, Bill seemed already to be slipping out of reach. Greg grabbed his shoulders and shook him . . . and at that point, realized that he was panicking and only wasting valuable time.

"Knife!" Greg almost sobbed the word out, and having gotten that much of his senses together, he remembered that there was a snakebite kit in Thisbe's pack. He swung the light toward Beebe, and seeing him bent over and sick, knew he would have to do it by himself.

But before he could move, Bill slowly sat up, groaning and trembling like an old man. His fingers pushed and tested along his side, and a faint, bewildered smile crept into his face. He took a deep breath and said, "You aren't going to do any cutting on me."

"But we have to!" Greg argued. "Got to get the poison out!"

"No . . . I was just scared. All I need is to rest a minute." And knowing they still did not understand, he lifted his arm to reveal the tear in his shirt. It was wet with venom, but on his bare ribs beneath, there

62

was no sign of a bite. "See? He was just caught in my shirt . . ."

Greg stood up, feeling weak. "I thought for sure . . ."

"So did I . . . and that close to the heart, I probably would've died. But my *shirt!*" Very quietly Bill began to laugh. And for one of the few times in his life, it was close to crying.

"Man!" Beebe shook his head, but could not turn and look at them. "Oh, *man* . . ." And that about summed it up.

They waited for a few minutes, long enough for Bill to pull himself together. Then, more slowly than ever, they moved on through the nightmare.

The boys did not know how long it was before the stink and the sound began to diminish and fall behind. But while they had remembered, somewhere in their paralyzed spirits, that there had to be another side, it was still startling to break out of stone and go hurrying along the ridge.

Given the measure of the earth's turning, not much time had passed. The western horizon was still a narrow wash of blue. But back there, where life had been uncertain, time was within and different . . . its smallest particle hinted of eternity. And so, to this other evening, they came drained of all but the surprise of having survived. The three did not talk about what had happened, even after they moved down the ridge and stopped, deep in the softness of redwoods.

9.

The sixth morning was one of gray and somber mists. There in the redwoods, in that dim and uncertain light where ferns and towering trees seemed to sleep and wait, it could have been not just the dawn of a day, but the dawning of time as well.

The boys built the fire up and huddled around it for breakfast, not really looking forward to the dismal business of breaking a wet camp.

"The fog ought to burn off by ten or so," Beebe said. "Why not wait and get everything dried out before we go? I sure don't like the idea of damp sleeping bags tonight."

"We can do that when we stop at noon," Greg replied. "It's better not to lose any more time than we have to."

"Might not be fog . . ." Bill studied the dripping branches far above them.

"What's the matter, Greg?" Beebe asked. "You still worried about Morgan?"

"No. I'm sure he thinks we came to a sudden end last night."

Beebe shuddered. "Wow, that was bad news! How many do you suppose there were, Bill?"

The Modoc stirred the fire. "I don't know. Probably not as many as we thought."

"Maybe a thousand," Beebe said.

Bill laughed at him. "Nah . . . I figured two hundred at most. Maybe less."

"Now just because you're an Indian doesn't mean you . . ." Beebe began, his voice edged with sudden irritation. But he stopped, visibly surprised at himself.

Greg stood up. "Let's kill the fire and get moving."

It took half an hour to put the packs in order and get rolling again. Shortly after that, they came to a break in the trees and discovered that Bill's suspicions had been correct. It was not fog that had been dripping off the trees, but a slow, fine rain. Unless it blew over, they were in for a miserable day. Not having anticipated bad weather during that time of year and wanting to restrict their packs to the absolute necessities, they had not included raincoats or ponchos. The best they could manage were nylon windbreakers, which were lined and warm but would shed rain only for a little while.

The rain made a dark place darker, and soaked to the skin before they were an hour out of camp, the boys became dispirited and silent. Even the mules seemed

65

burdened by the day; limp-eared and reluctant, they would not hold the pace long without being pulled.

Beebe jerked at Thisbe. "Come on, you miserable . . ."

"Take it easy," Greg said.

"Who pushed your button?"

"Look, Beebe, things are bad enough," Greg told him, "without you taking it out on a dumb animal."

"Dumb?" Bill snorted. "Turn them loose and they'll head for home. That's how dumb *they* are!"

"That's for sure." Beebe grumbled. "This whole thing is dumb. Wandering around out here . . . what's it got us? A crazy man with a shotgun and a mountain full of rattlesnakes! And why?"

"*Sasquatch!*" Bill made a face and walked like Frankenstein's monster.

"You two didn't have to come," Greg said quietly. "But you sure were whistling a different tune the other night when you thought something was moving around in the moonlight. I'm getting fed up with both of you."

"It's mutual!" Beebe spat it out.

"Well, I'll tell you what," Greg said. "We're close to the Oregon border and the Elk Valley Forest Service Station . . . and that's where good old Highway 199 cuts across our route. So if you want to hitch a ride and go home, it's okay with me."

Nothing more was said for several minutes. Each went into himself, and it was hard to come out again. But, though clearly uncomfortable, Bill West finally broke the silence.

66

"It's just the rain."

"Sure." Beebe was embarrassed. "I know."

Just the rain . . . Greg watched the ancient giants rising about them, and wondered . . .

Three miles after leaving the Six Rivers country and entering the Siskiyou National Forest, they crossed the highway. It was strange to see, strange to feel it underfoot . . . and stranger still to enter the forest again and hear, behind them, the rumble of a passing truck.

"Feels almost crowded around here," Greg observed.

"Well, you white people had to go start a population explosion, didn't you!" Bill said.

It was good to laugh, but the feeling did not last long. That slow, drizzling rain had gradually turned heavy. It pounded and hammered at their spirits until they were as weary and depressed as ever. Greg supposed it was only because they were tired, but the rain seemed colder now. In spite of their exertion, they had become chilled.

Greg finally called a halt. They rigged a tarp for shelter, and after considerable coaxing, got a fire going. Breaking from the usual midday pattern, they ate a hot meal and drank large amounts of scalding tea. To some extent, the boys were even able to dry their clothes. But it was only a momentary comfort. As soon as the journey was resumed, it would all be the same again.

"There's one good thing." Greg was watching the water pouring off the tarp. "If Bigfoot crosses our path in the next couple of days, we sure have a better chance of finding footprints."

No more than a mile later, as if Greg had been prophetic, they found tracks.

It was startling, to say the least. Forgetting the rain, the boys gathered around the prints and, for a time, could only stare. The ground was far too soft to retain detail, but the traces were quite large and new enough to be still crumbling around the edges. The creature that made them had gone uphill from there, and Bill glanced quickly in that direction.

"What do you think?" Beebe asked.

"Let's tether the mules," Greg said, "and see if we can catch up with it."

Beebe straightened up. "You're kidding!"

"This is what we came for, isn't it?"

Making sure his camera was ready, but leaving it in the case to stay dry, Greg hurried along the tracks and began to climb, with Bill and Beebe close behind. And it was an uncomfortable thing. Unlike the night Beebe saw something, there was time here to think and to watch themselves *deliberately* moving in the direction of . . . what? Judging from the tracks, their quarry was only minutes away, somewhere among the trees above them. Hurrying, their progress muffled by driving rain, they were bound to catch up.

In that muted light of clouds, forest and rain-darkened wood, Greg was near the limit of his lens. Knowing that both he and his subject might be in motion

68

when the moment came, he had set the shutter speed at 250. Even with the film's ASA rating boosted to 1600, it meant using an aperture of f2. That was all right . . . good, in fact, for separating his target from a busy background. But a shallow depth of field was also unforgiving when it came to errors in focusing, and it worried him.

You're going to be sweating and out of breath, he told himself, and excited . . . maybe afraid . . . you know there isn't going to be much time. Three or four seconds at most . . . and the eyepiece is going to start steaming up as soon as you look through it. With all that going on, you're supposed to snap the lens into sharp focus! Sure . . . and keep it there . . .

Greg could not help remembering what Beverly had said about having to shoot instinctively. He wondered now if he had the necessary instincts. Circumstances considered, it did not seem likely that there would be much else in his favor.

The time for worrying about it ran out. Above them, maybe fifty yards away, there was a vague flurry of motion as something quickly moved into sight and out again . . . too quickly to leave more than a dim impression. Greg dug his toes into that steep slope and picked up the pace. Ten minutes more, maybe. And it was hard. His lungs were already beginning to burn with the effort.

But only a moment passed before Bill groaned and grabbed at Greg's arm. "Forget it . . . just a bear."

"What?"

"Up near the top . . . to the left . . . see him?"

Looking where Bill pointed, Greg saw it, then . . . an ordinary bear silhouetted against the sky.

"Sorry about that," he said. "Guess I had you guys running for nothing."

"So what else is new?" Beebe grumbled.

They headed back down to the mules, and with the perspective that comes of calm, Greg had to admit that the tracks were not large enough. And Bill noticed now with some consternation that while the bear must have walked upright, leaving the creek, the pattern of its prints going uphill was that of a four-legged animal.

"As an Indian, I make a great fork-lift operator."

The presence of the bear indicated a nearness to a more open kind of forest, since the redwoods did not support life of any kind. It was a temptation to follow the bear's example and put this place behind for something less dark and gloomy. But the three were too tired to make the climb, and so they continued in that rain-filled twilight.

Perhaps something of those unexpected tracks remained in the back of their minds to nag, but as they moved slowly and wearily toward evening, the rain was full of ghosts . . . images and furtive shapes twisting and turning in the shifting curtains before them. But like secrets in a bad dream, they never came into clear view.

That night, beneath a fallen redwood, Bill managed to find enough dry wood to get a fire going. Under the

70

tarp, they warmed and dried themselves, ate a simple meal, and gradually began to feel more like themselves. But turning in, and on the edge of sleep, it was too easy to remember the ghosts in the rain . . .

10.

The rain went away sometime during the night, and the water dripping from the trees slowed and came to silence. The morning was the seventh of the expedition; the halfway point. It was one of broken clouds and brilliant intervals of sun. The boys proclaimed a morning of rest in which they would stay put and do a little housekeeping.

Their clothes, dry but stiff with dirt, were washed in the stream and hung before a blazing fire. Cooking gear was given more than a hasty wipe, sleeping bags were shaken out and aired, boots were cleaned and oiled, trash was burned, and the cans, which had to be taken along, were flattened and bundled. Pyramus and Thisbe was given a rubdown and an extra ration of barley.

By noon, the expedition bore some resemblance to

the way it looked the day it left Middlefork. They packed up and resumed the journey then, moving south of two peaks called The Lieutenants, and east of El Capitan and Copper Mountain. They had traded the Siskiyou for the Klamath National Forest.

There were no bears and no rain ghosts to nag at them. They were in high spirits, and the afternoon was very calm and peaceful.

The change that came over the camp late that night was slow. It was no more to be noticed than the slight bending of grass that whispers of a gentle wind. The fire burned low. The boys had been in their sleeping bags for only a few minutes. Close to the edge of sleep, they were barely aware of the restlessness that began to touch Pyramus and Thisbe. The mules sighed and shuffled, and seemed to resent their tethers. And as if there were some kind of electricity in the air, the skin along their spines rippled and twitched.

Like a gnat's whine, it was nothing, and yet something. What the mules were doing seemed without reason or importance, but it persisted and nagged until Bill sat up to watch them.

"What's the matter with those clowns?" Greg groaned.

"Don't know . . . politicking for more barley, maybe. I might as well give them a little more. But we're going to run low if we don't start grazing them more often."

Bill crawled out and barefooted it to the supplies to

73

throw a few handfuls of the grain into a couple of pans. Giving it to the mules, he went back to his sleeping bag and settled down again.

Except for the grinding sound of their broad molars, Pyramus and Thisbe were quiet once more.

"Glad they don't eat celery!" Beebe grumbled and turned over, trying to sleep.

But it did not last long. In that warm, vague time when the boys were just drifting off, the mules started shuffling again and testing the air. Greg rose up on one elbow and saw that their ears were erect and alert. Following their line of attention, he noticed shadows of clouds scudding across the moon. He supposed they did not understand the interplay of light and dark out in that open space. Or perhaps it was a bear or mountain lion passing somewhere near camp. But seeing nothing himself, Greg relaxed and closed his eyes, too sleepy to care.

Even the thick folds of the bag were not enough to mask it . . . the sharp snapping of twigs that suddenly had the mules jerking hard at their tethers. Greg sat up and found Bill already out of his bag, crouching there and listening.

"Something's here," the Indian whispered. With a gesture he warned Beebe, who was still half asleep, to be quiet.

Very carefully they slipped their boots on, and Greg got the camera, stuffing extra flashbulbs in his shirt pocket.

"See anything?" Beebe whispered.

"Not yet," Greg told him. "Twigs snapped . . . mules are pretty upset."

"Should've put our food away," Bill said. "Might be a bear sniffing around.

Greg nodded and nudged Beebe. "But you better be ready with that can of oil."

It soon became obvious that something was approaching camp. Gripping the camera tightly to keep his hands from shaking, Greg moved away from the fire so that he could see better, and Bill went to the mules hoping to calm them.

Now, it was mere yards away, just beyond the reach of firelight. It was large, whatever it was . . . very large! Estimating the distance to be somewhere between forty and fifty feet, Greg set his lens at the infinity mark. He would not have to worry about focus until their visitor came within thirty feet.

Watching through the lens and hearing the mules becoming more and more distressed, Greg saw a light-edged shadow move across one corner of his field of vision. He moved the camera to catch it, but resisted the impulse to press the shutter button. Closer, he thought . . . let it get a little closer . . . at that distance the trees will soak up a lot of the flash . . . and relax . . . try to relax.

It seemed headed for the mules, judging by the sound of its approach. And so Greg picked a group of trees that seemed to be in that line of travel and tried his best to bring them into focus. It was too dark for him to do more than guess. But he was hoping the smaller aperture allowed by the flash would cancel any error involved. He was tempted to close the aperture another two stops to increase the depth of field. Underexposed film could be intensified during development. The result was limited, mostly a matter of increased contrast, but . . . *stop it! Quit fussing and relax!*

A moment later, the time for thinking was gone. The mules were going mad, and it was obvious that their visitor had come much closer. Greg saw something move out from behind a tree and hesitate . . . the image was dim and ill defined but gave the impression of such size that he did not think about the camera until it was too late. That opportunity missed, he had to wait for the thing to reappear and then began shooting as fast as he could change flashbulbs. But at *what?* Greg did not know what Beebe and the Indian were seeing when the flashes went off. Because a mirror had to flip out of the way, to expose the film, his viewfinder blacked out at the instant of illumination. He never really saw what he was shooting at . . . just a vague kind of shadow moving through the trees. To make matters worse now, its position was such that Bill and the lunging mules kept getting in the way.

Needing badly to get a clear, uninterrupted shot, Greg ran to one side, but it was too late. At that same moment, the mules finally broke free and went stampeding off into the dark. And just as suddenly, their intruder seemed no longer in evidence.

Not taking time to think about it, Greg hurried into the dark. The best he could do was watch the patches of moonlight and wait for shape or motion to be silhouetted against them. He saw something moving almost immediately and stepped toward it to get a closer shot. Setting the lens to its smallest aperture, he raised the camera and tried to focus . . . but something went wrong. Alarmed or slowed too much by the trees, the creature stopped and turned. Greg was not aware of it until it loomed above him and blotted out the moonlight . . .

He tried to back off, but there was a deep growling sound, and the briefest impression of being struck on the side of the head.

"You're crazy!"

It was the first thing Greg heard, when he stirred and opened his eyes.

"What were you trying to do, go home in a box?" Bill's relief spilled over into sarcasm.

Greg sucked in some air and dared move a little more. "Better than walking . . ."

"I don't know about you photo-gophers," Bill grumbled. "So how do you feel?"

"How big a truck was it!" He groaned, deciding against sitting up.

Bill nodded, knowingly. "I'm not surprised. You've been out almost forty minutes. Can you move your head? Arms, legs . . ."

Greg moved everything, slowly and painfully. "Any damage?"

"Well, guess nothing's broken. But one ear might

catch fire, and you're going to have a dandy bruise. Beebe, get me a towel and some cold water. Maybe we can keep your eye from swelling shut . . ."

"What did you see?" Greg asked, as Bill started applying cold compresses. "Anything?"

"Just something moving. After you started firing flashbulbs, all I saw was big green spots!"

Greg turned his head a little to find Beebe. "How about you?"

Bill snorted. "All he saw was a tree. Up close!"

"What he means," Beebe mumbled, "is that I hid behind a tree."

"Oh . . ." Greg said, and considering his own condition, added, "I'm not sure I blame you."

Bill spat with disgust. "But he should've been by the fire with the oil! What if that thing had come into camp?"

Unable to speak, Beebe shuffled away from the fire. He sat down near the supplies, his head on his knees.

Bill started to say something else, but Greg stopped him. "Take it easy."

"But it's the *third* time he's folded! If he's going to do that every time things get rough . . ."

"I know, Bill. But he can't help it . . . he's more upset about it than you are. This trip just isn't his bag. But we didn't know that and neither did he. We'll have to make allowances and do the best we can, that's all."

"You're right." Bill slowly stood up. After a minute, he said, "No need to sit out there, Beebe . . . sorry I lost my temper."

"I had it coming," Beebe muttered. "But, thanks anyway . . . I'll be over in a little while."

Trying to get away from the awkwardness of the moment, Greg finally said, "So . . . all you saw was big green spots. I wonder why the thing kept coming. You'd think the flashes would scare it off."

"I thought about that," Bill said, putting another compress on. "It must've seemed like lightning. And animals aren't afraid of it."

That made a certain amount of sense, but Greg was already trying to remember something else.

"Tell me something," he said to Bill. "When we first heard it coming, you said something about a bear sniffing around . . . and it was a possibility."

"Yes," Bill agreed. "So?"

"Well, when a bear thinks it's being attacked and takes a swing at something, what are the chances of *not* being clawed?"

"Pretty small, I'd say."

"Okay . . . so do I have any cuts or scratches on my head? Is there *anything* besides a bruise?"

"No," Bill told him. "Nothing."

"Don't you see? It doesn't prove anything, and maybe I'm wrong . . . but I don't think this thing had claws."

"Suggesting that it was Bigfoot," Bill said.

Greg nodded.

With that, they fell silent. Beebe rejoined them, putting more wood on the fire to keep it burning high, and Bill continued treating Greg's bruise. The night seemed peaceful enough now, but there was not one of them who did not occasionally stare out into the darkness and question the quiet.

"The mules didn't come back, did they?" Greg said, finally.

"No," Bill replied. "But there's no point in going after them until morning."

"Maybe they'll wander in before then," Beebe decided.

"After the scare they got here, I doubt it," Bill said. "I just hope they slowed down after the first hundred miles."

And so they went on waiting and wondering, and after a while, watched for morning in the sky . . .

11.

When dawn was more than a thin gray spirit lost behind the high ridges, and the boys could begin to see their own part of the forest, they laced their boots tight, and not taking time to eat, followed after the mules. None of them spoke. That dim morning of dark trees and clouds might yet hide what had come to them in the night, and not knowing the nature of it, they were wary. Saying nothing, they could also listen for the slightest sound that might betray the whereabouts of Pyramus and Thisbe.

It was not hard, at first, to follow where sharp hoofs had gouged and torn the soft, carpeted earth. But, perhaps a mile out of camp, the traces became faint. Here, the mules' terror had eased and they had stopped running. But the dim crescent marks continued in the same direction and showed no indication of turning back in the direction of camp.

"What do you think, Bill?" Beebe asked.

"Well, the thing wasn't chasing them. At least not along the line we've been following. I don't think anything like Bigfoot, if that's what it was, could run fast enough. Over a short distance, a *bear* could outrun a mule . . . but there hasn't been any sign of a fight. No, if they were being chased at all, it wasn't for long. By the time the mules got here, they were tired and the smell of the thing was out of their nostrils. But they were still afraid enough to go on putting distance between themselves and camp."

"And so," Greg guessed, "we still have a long walk ahead of us."

"They've had most of the night to travel," Bill said, "but that doesn't have to mean anything. We might find them turning back in a little while . . . or just standing somewhere, waiting. And there's another thing in our favor . . . their stomachs. If there's an open field anywhere ahead of us in the next couple of miles, we'll probably find them there."

On this encouraging note, the three continued to follow the thin trace. It was fortunate, though predictable, that Pyramus and Thisbe stayed together. And so was their tendency to take the line of least resistance; their way led up, down and around, but never challenged the mountains. Not encountering any hard and tiring climbs, the boys were able to sustain a pace that gave them a better chance of overtaking the mules.

Sometimes the tracks were so faint that they seemed old . . . as if they had been there, undisturbed, for years. And often, they seemed so fresh that the boys were certain they were going to find the animals within a matter of minutes . . . but the mules were never there to put an end to the search.

As the pursuit continued far into the morning, the boys became increasingly anxious. Without the mules, the expedition was finished. And worse, they would be faced with the difficulty of carrying enough food on their own backs to reach home again.

But if there was ever a chance to overtake the animals, it was lost to rain. It came before noon. Reaching cloudburst proportions at times, the rain wiped out the last of those fragile tracks.

Bill insisted that they keep going for a while longer, just to give the search one more chance. But there was nothing to follow, and they could not see much more than themselves in the downpour. And so there was no choice, finally, but to turn around and go back.

There were times of doubt in that rain-lost world, times when what might have been expected or remembered was gone . . . a certain tree, a rock, the run of a hill. But Bill led them downward and straight until they inevitably found the creek. It was a wandering and longer way, and yet one that, sooner or later, would take them where they had to go.

When the boys reached camp in the middle of the afternoon, chilled and weary, and with the rain still coming hard, they looked around and refused to believe, at first, that it had been destroyed . . .

12.

The boys wandered aimlessly through the destruction. They did not yet consider a cause, but tried to comprehend and accept the fact of it. And the fact was that very little of the supplies and equipment had escaped that nameless whirlwind. The little primus stove was smashed and the packsaddles were shattered; most of their tin plates and cups had been damaged, the big battery light was useless, and their gallon canteen had been flattened. As for their food supplies, anything that was in a box or bag had been opened and scattered to be ground into the mud or spoiled by the rain. Though it was hard to tell in that mess, some of it appeared to have been eaten or stolen . . . things like fruit bars and chocolate. Even the canned goods, already depleted, had not entirely escaped. Some of the cans, subjected to great weight or strength, had literally exploded.

Beebe walked a few yards toward the trees and

picked up the camera tripod. It had been bent double. "Greg?"

"Oh Lord . . ." Remembering his three-hundred dollar camera, and feeling sick inside, Greg got down on his knees to search through all that mess.

"Here," Bill said, lifting the sodden remains of a sleeping bag. "It looks all right . . . the other lens, too."

Greg examined the camera and the 135mm lens; both were wet but otherwise unharmed. The plastic bag containing the cans of exposed film was also intact.

There was nothing to be done except stretch a tarp for a lean-to and wait for the rain to stop. Bill found the boot oil and used it to start some small wood burning, and with that he built a bigger fire. They brewed some strong tea in one of the surviving cooking pots and sat there wondering at it all.

"What do you suppose it was?" Beebe asked.

"Our friend from last night," Greg replied. "What else?"

Beebe shrugged. "I don't know, but I've seen bears do this in parks . . . you know, to tourists."

"That happens," Bill agreed, "but it isn't the same."

Beebe looked at him. "What's different about it?"

"A bear comes into a camp looking for food . . . he makes a mess and does the damage it takes to get at what he wants. That's all. But what about a doubled-up tripod and that big flashlight and the primus stove. That's not a search for food . . . that's pure *anger!*"

Greg nodded, gingerly touching the side of his head

where a large bruise was beginning to turn dark. "Bigfoot," he said. "I'm sure of it."

"We'll know when you develop the film," Beebe said.

"Hopefully," Greg answered. "In the meantime, I think we have a problem . . . unless the mules come back."

Bill threw more wood on the fire. "Don't hold your breath. They have a bad thing to remember here. We'll stay until tomorrow, just in case . . . have to, anyway, this late. But we better get all the canned goods together and see what we have left and how much we can carry."

Beebe frowned. "Cans will be heavy, even divided three ways . . . and it won't add up to a lot of food."

"That's the problem," Greg said. "We're not only going to be limited in what we can carry, but I think it's pretty obvious we'll have to ration our food if it's going to last all the way back to Middlefork."

They sat for a while, reluctant to get wet again. But Bill finally stretched. "Might as well get some of this in order."

"Before we do," Greg said, "let me grab a picture."

Bill was clearly annoyed. "Why did you wait until now?"

"I was wet and tired too! Besides, I've been looking . . . and I can't get enough in at one time unless I stand on something."

"On the big stool we didn't bring?" Bill suggested.

"I was thinking about Beebe helping me."

"Me!" Beebe eyes widened. "You want to stand on *me?*"

"Your shoulders. I wouldn't ask, except it's important. How about it? I'll even take my boots off."

Dismally, Beebe shook his head. "Let's get it over with."

He found the angle he wanted and removed his boots. Beebe had to kneel so that Greg could sit on his shoulders. "Okay Beebe, take it easy. Don't need any hernias on this trip."

Beebe said something about elephants and slowly unfolded until he stood erect. Unpracticed in such gymnastics, Greg had trouble getting the first foot up on Beebe's shoulder. The second was easier, but they swayed dangerously.

"You guys . . ." Bill howled hysterically, "oughta be on TV!"

Planting his feet wider, Beebe managed to stabilize the situation. "Now Greg!" He grunted. "Do it now!"

Holding his breath and trying to relax, Greg put the viewfinder to his eye and quickly framed what he wanted. "Got it!"

Beebe stood like an impatient telephone pole until Greg was down again. "Anything else? A doormat or something?"

Bill left the fire then, and still grinning, said, "Let's take care of the canned goods first."

It was a wet and miserable job, searching through all that mess and gathering up the cans. More than thirty minutes passed before they found the last one and added it to the pile.

"Less than I thought," Bill said.

"Yeah." Greg was not surprised. "But how many times did we eat out of cans because we couldn't be bothered with the other?"

Bill wiped his face. "I know. Well . . . tomorrow we'll sort it out. Unless there's room, no point in carrying juice or soup, or things like fruit and condensed milk. First choice has to be the solid things like beans and meat."

The next item was to dry a tarp to use in place of the ruined sleeping bags. And while they were propping it up near the fire, Greg remembered something and looked toward the forest.

"You know what?" he said. "We didn't look for footprints!"

"Wasn't time." Bill opened some cans of sliced peaches. "It was more important to find the mules. And there was no way of knowing it was going to rain like that. Anyway, if you got Bigfoot on film, that's all that really matters."

"That's true," Greg said. "But just the same . . ."

Bill put the peaches in a pan and held it over the fire. "Sure, it would've been great to see them."

Beebe stared at the pan. "What're you doing?"

"Frying peaches," Bill told him.

"You mean the rationing begins tonight? Right *now?*"

"That's the general idea, Beebe, but it'll be sweet, hot and filling enough to get to sleep on."

"Yeah, *sure* it will . . ."

"Okay Beebe, take the pan," Bill told him.

"Why?"

"Well, rather than have you suffer like that, I thought I'd run down to the nearest grocery store and buy you a nice big steak."

"All right," Beebe mumbled. "I got the message."

And so they ate and settled back under canvas loud with rain. There was little more to be said. What might be on the film and getting back to Middlefork . . . that was all that was really important now.

The rain finally came to an end sometime after midnight, and a single star winked down through the trees. By then, the slow drying of the tarp was done, and the boys wrapped in it and somehow drifted off to sleep . . .

13.

It was still dark when a hand shook Greg out of a dream, and he found Bill leaning over him. Wondering at the blackness, he looked at his watch and found that it was only a little after three o'clock.

"What's the matter?" he mumbled and rolled over. "Not time to get up . . ."

Bill would not let him go back to sleep but shook him again. "We've got something . . . hear it?"

Greg came up on one elbow and listened beyond his own breathing to the sound of the creek, and then beyond that . . . and heard, not too far away, a sharp, high-pitched barking.

"Dog?" He asked it before he remembered how remote they were from where even a far-roaming dog would be.

"No . . . I thought it was a coyote or fox . . . but I've been listening for a couple of hours now. And it's like a fox . . . but it isn't . . ."

"Isn't?" Greg, who had never heard a fox bark, sat up to listen more carefully. "In what way?"

"Don't know," the Modoc whispered, and hunkered down by the fire. "Just *different*. And it stays in one place . . . a fox would be hunting now and on the move. And he wouldn't be giving himself away with all that noise."

Greg began to feel a chill. "Would a coyote?"

"No . . . a fox and a coyote are like brothers . . . same kind of thing."

Greg listened for a while longer to a sound buried in the deeps of forest and night. Then he turned to the Indian, the chill becoming a tightness along his spine.

"Bigfoot's come back," he said. "That what you're thinking?"

"Anybody know what Sasquatch is supposed to sound like?"

"No . . . I don't think so," Greg replied. "But . . ."

"But what?"

"Trying to think . . . maybe a movie I saw. I don't know, but it seems to me the big apes can make barking noises. And there *is* a resemblance between apes and Bigfoot. They might sound alike."

Bill shrugged. "Makes sense."

"Maybe we ought to get Beebe up . . ."

"What he doesn't know won't scare him to death," Bill said and then sighed, as if to apologize. "No . . . let him sleep. You want to try for a picture, just in case?"

Greg thought about it and was tempted but shook

his head. "I don't think there's any chance of getting close enough without being heard . . . don't even know its exact location. And if that *is* Bigfoot, I sure don't want to get flattened again. I think there's a better chance for pictures if he comes to us."

"That's how I see it," Bill agreed.

Readying his camera and flash unit, Greg crawled back under the canvas. "If I can stay awake . . ."

"We better sleep," Bill said.

"But . . ."

"If it stops barking, I'll wake up."

Greg wondered at that. "Old Indian trick?"

"Sure! And if you have a deck of cards, I'll show you another." Bill grinned, then turning serious, said, "I don't know what it is . . . don't know why. But sudden quiet is like a noise to me . . ."

Greg reached out for that deep place, tried with his mind to see what night and distance kept hidden. Maybe it was only some harsh-throated bird, awakened by hunger and quarreling with the persistent dark . . . he had not thought to ask, and Bill was already asleep. Bigfoot? Maybe that huge man-thing *had* returned . . . but why? To wait and watch for them to leave, to consider once again those puny beings that were, in some unsettling way, a little like himself? It was an uneasy thing, not knowing what to expect. And yet, without realizing it, Greg closed his eyes and drifted away . . .

14.

Greg stirred slowly and uncertainly, remaining behind closed eyes to drift back and forth between awareness and the edge of sleep. Then, with some quick sparking of memory, he sat up suddenly to blink at the daylight. He looked at Bill and found him awake, and the Indian answered a wordless question with a shake of his head.

"It left," Bill said, getting up. "At dawn. Barking got farther away. I couldn't hear it any more."

Greg stared red-eyed into nothing and did not really care. He just sat there, not even hearing Beebe's groaning protests at being awakened.

This ninth morning had given them silent and drifting fog, a dismal and discouraging beginning. The boys were cold and stiff from lying on wet ground. Their clothes were too damp to give warmth, and fitful sleep had not held much rest. Worse, last night's fire

93

was now only blackened wood and useless ash. And as if all that were not enough, a small hope had died. Pyramus and Thisbe had not come back to regain, in that wilderness, the familiar company of man. What was left of the expedition had to be put in order, somehow, and the long journey home begun. But they could only stand there trembling, as if already defeated.

It was Bill West who, studying the forest around them, finally snapped out of apathy and began to function. He disappeared for fifteen or twenty minutes and came back carrying an armload of dry wood. Shortly, he had the beginnings of a fire, which he nursed carefully until it generated enough heat to get the wet wood going.

"Where in the world did you find it?" Greg asked him.

"Goose pens," Bill said.

"What?" Beebe was puzzled.

"Goose pens," Bill told him. "You've seen them. The redwoods that have been hollowed out by fire. I guess the first settlers sometimes kept their geese in them."

The pens, Greg remembered, were often the size of small rooms, blackened and charred. And yet, almost miraculously, these ancient scars were in the hearts of living trees.

"It's funny," Greg said, beginning to cheer up a little.

"Something's *funny?*" Beebe grumbled.

"The wood Bill brought back . . . do you realize

94

how old it might be? I mean, it's not like the usual dead stuff you find under trees. This was inside the pens . . . the wind had to be blowing in just a certain way, or the branch had to bounce just right. And you know redwood doesn't rot like other wood. Insects won't touch it. Well, it's just funny to think about starting a fire with wood that might be four or five hundred years old."

Beebe frowned into a cup of tea. "Man, this has been some trip! We go chasing after hairy monsters, wind up in front of a shotgun, run into half the snakes in California, and then something comes and wipes us out . . . and now all you can think about is how old the kindling is! What next?"

Greg grinned at him. "Well, we had a visitor last night. Something that barked like a fox but wasn't a fox and . . ."

"Wait!" Beebe groaned. "I've changed my mind! I don't want to know!"

Greg shrugged. "Doesn't matter. We don't know what it was, and it's gone anyway."

After a while, warmed and dried by the fire, and with a breakfast of fried pineapple under their belts, they started sorting the canned goods into three piles, trying to figure out what they could carry. According to Greg's estimate, they had roughly thirty-five miles between them and home, allowing for the demands of the terrain. It meant cutting west across the middle of what had been the expedition's circular route.

"Four days' food?" Greg suggested.

"No," Bill replied. "This stuff will slow us down at first. Make it six . . . and even at that, like you said, we ought to ration ourselves."

Beebe was skeptical. *"Six* days for thirty-five miles?"

"Okay, so if we make better time, we can have a feast on our last day out," Bill admitted. "But I don't think we ought to take chances. We carry what we can, and we go as far as we can each day . . . *without* breaking our backs. It won't accomplish anything if we burn ourselves up in the first fifteen miles."

Greg added extra cans to allow for the six-day estimate and stood up. "Well, unless I've overdone it, looks like we won't be leaving anything but a few cans of juice and fruit . . . look okay?"

Bill weighed the piles in his mind. "Sure. Beebe?"

"If a runty Modoc can carry it, so can I!"

The next step was to cut one of the canvas tarps into three pieces. These they fashioned into crude back packs; to keep them from cutting into their shoulders, the ropes were wrapped and padded with cloth taken from clothing that had to be discarded.

When the packs were loaded with the canned goods, they added a few necessary extras . . . a pot, three cups, forks, a can opener and a box of matches. Beebe and Bill divided these items between them. Greg took the map and his camera gear and a tightly rolled tarp for shelter.

They were ready, now. But Bill looked around and said, "Let's don't leave it this way."

Greg and Beebe agreed without having to say a

word. It meant delaying another hour, perhaps. Not leaving litter behind them had been a rule of the expedition. But it was more than that now. In a way, it was a means of starting over, or at least of being able to meet trouble with a clear slate.

And so they burned what they could and stacked the rest in a neat pile. This they covered with canvas which they weighted down with rocks. It was the best they could do.

Killing the fire, then, they shouldered their packs and quietly walked away.

If they had felt any optimism about setting a good pace and getting the miles behind them quickly, it was soon lost to the reality of the packs and a bad night's sleep. Even though they had started late, it seemed unreasonable to come to noon and find little more than a mile behind them.

And that fog . . . instead of burning off in the late morning or early afternoon, as was most often the case, it persisted and drifted across the Siskiyou Mountains in a heavy gray blanket. Indeed, the fog obscured the tops of mountains like Bearpaw, Prescott and Jedediah, and in so doing, robbed them of the landmarks that would have given certainty to their navigation. Depending entirely on the map was risky; its detail was not so complete that they could count on following the right creek. Greg had a compass, naturally, but the reading it gave would be the same on both sides of a mountain, which meant they could be going in the right direction in the wrong canyon, a mistake that could cost them precious time. It was a possibility that constantly nagged.

But more than that, it was simply gray and wet . . . the dark forest was darker with it. It was so depressing that one could beg for the sight of something red or yellow. All they could see was gray green and gray brown, and the lifeless wet gray of the sky. Their minds grew heavy with it and their thoughts inevitably returned to the morning's fire.

It was two o'clock when Beebe said, "Let's build a fire and have some tea. I'm due for a breather."

"Take too much time to find dry wood," Bill told him. "You can hold on a while longer."

"You found wood easily enough this morning," Beebe protested.

The Modoc kept on going. "I haven't seen a goose pen for the last mile or two."

"Okay, okay." Beebe was sounding rather edgy. "But let's at least stop and rest awhile. These ropes are getting to me."

Glancing back, Greg said, "Looks like you didn't pad them enough."

"Yeah? Well I guess I'm just not a good boy scout like you and that . . . you two!" Beebe almost shouted at them.

Bill stopped and turned around. "That *what?*"

"Nothing. Lay off!"

Puzzled, Greg also stopped. "Just what *is* it with you, Beebe? Take it easy."

"Sure!" Beebe slipped the pack off and sat down. "Maybe if you had a few more cans instead of that camera stuff you're carrying, you wouldn't be so eager-beaver about going on."

Greg went back, frowning, to confront Beebe. "That doesn't make sense," Greg said. "You know the cans were divided equally. My camera gear is extra weight . . . not to mention the tarp. For crying out loud, if you want to count to the last pound, I'm probably carrying more than you."

"Just forget it!" Beebe growled.

"No," Greg insisted. "If you've got too much, I'm sure Bill can handle a few extra cans. No point in . . ."

Beebe's hands began to tremble. "I said forget it!"

Greg shrugged out of his pack and motioned for Bill to do the same. "You've got a complaint. Let's straighten it out."

"Lots of luck!" Bill said.

"What did you say?" Beebe stood up.

"I said lots of luck! You'll shoot your mouth off, anyway!"

"Wait a minute, Bill." Greg touched his shoulder. "Wait . . ."

Bill let his breath out. "You're right. Sorry, Beebe . . . look, give me some of your cans so we can get moving."

"Nothing doing! I'm not so tired that I need help from a little red boy!"

Bill flinched but then settled into a different kind of

99

calm; the wrong kind. It was cold, metallic, and he had an odd smile. "So that's it . . . little *red* boy."

"Hey, come on, Beebe!" Greg stepped between them. "You two have been friends for a long time. He didn't mean it, Bill."

The expression on Bill's face did not change. "Sure he did. He wouldn't have thought it if he didn't. Well, how about it, Beebe? Mustn't strain yourself. Want to go piggy-back?"

Beebe yelled something unintelligible, pushed Greg aside and hit Bill hard enough to send him sprawling. The Modoc got up on his hands and knees, watched the other for an instant and came off the ground, cat-fast, springing to catch Beebe at the knees and bring him down. Almost in the same motion, Bill delivered two short jabs that started Beebe's nose bleeding. Twisting his long frame and pushing, Beebe broke loose and drove his fist into Bill's stomach. He jumped to his feet, staggered back to get his balance and then rushed Bill to keep the advantage. But the Indian came up too fast, and stepping aside, caught Beebe with a two-handed chop on the back of his neck that sent him crashing to the ground again.

Greg grabbed Bill and tried to stop him, only to have Beebe come up from behind, swinging blindly to get at the Indian. One of the blows caught Greg on the side of his head. His knees buckled, and in that moment of having to defend himself, it became a free-for-all. And it did not stop until he picked Bill up to throw him back for a few feet and whirled around to face

Beebe with one hand out for a warning and the other cocked to deliver a punch.

"That's enough, Beebe! You too, Bill! You've had your fun! Now cut it out before you really hurt each other!"

As if a light had been turned on, and the two were recognizing each other for the first time, the thing stopped. Bill and Beebe wandered away in opposite directions and sat down, surprised and breathing hard.

"Sorry," Bill said, finally.

Beebe stared at his knees. "No. I started it . . . don't know why."

They looked at each other with bewilderment. "It's crazy," Bill said. "We were like people I've never seen before."

Beebe kicked at a rock. "I guess it's just being tired and having bad luck. Maybe if the sun came out . . . we'd be okay."

After a pause Bill looked around at the forest. "I'm not so sure . . . don't you feel it?"

"The trees, you mean," Greg said.

Bill nodded. "Maybe I'm getting funny in the head, but it *is* the trees, isn't it?"

"I felt something strange," Greg almost whispered, "just before we crossed the highway up near the Oregon border . . . a feeling that something was working on us. It was like words without sound."

Beebe shuddered. "You act like they're not just trees but . . . well, *beings* of some kind."

"Maybe they are," Greg said.

101

"Aw come on!" Bill said. "That's going too far!"

"Maybe." Greg stretched out for a moment. "I don't know. But I read an article, not long ago, about a scientist who hooked up some kind of instrument to a potted plant . . . seems all living things have electricity in them. And when he threatened the plant with a pair of scissors, the instrument registered a violent reaction. So his theory is that plants have awareness of what's going on around them. Maybe the guy's a crackpot, and maybe he isn't. I don't know. But think about it . . . if a little thing like a flower has awareness, what about a two-thousand-year-old tree?"

"Too much for me," Bill admitted. "But something happens here. And I don't think we belong. Know what I mean?"

"Out of our natural element," Greg said. "Yes . . . and we can't let it get to us any more, if we're going to get home in one piece. What do you say we get going."

And so they shouldered their packs and moved on. Imagined or real, they felt hostility, something malignant in that shadowed place of giants . . .

15.

Late in the afternoon, the fog scattered in fugitive wisps and vanished. Far below that brilliant sky, the boys caught only thin shafts and flickerings of the sun. But their spirits soared, and their packs seemed lighter. With the sun, however, something else had come into that green silence. A dim sound . . . a whisper in the forest of a far and constant thunder.

They stopped, listening, and strained to give it a name. Fire, wind, the raging of a sea . . . they were too far from the Pacific to hear it, and a wind's voice was never that steady . . . and fire? It seemed to them that if they could hear a fire, they would also be able to smell it. And after all that rain and fog, a fire was highly unlikely anyway. *What,* then? But it was too thin and too nearly lost to know, and so the boys went on.

"I wish those mules would show up," Beebe said.

"They won't," Greg replied. "Not now. Rope bothering you again?"

"No, it isn't that. I was just thinking . . . we're going to have to pay for the mules. How much, do you suppose?"

"A few hundred, I guess. I don't know. Never bought any mules," Greg told him. "Even used ones."

Beebe smiled. "Pyramus and Thisbe were a couple of all right characters. I hope they're okay."

"Should be," Bill said. "Plenty of water in these mountains and enough to eat."

The sound seemed a little louder now, but there was no direction to it. They could not listen to the east or south, or any point of the compass, and say that that was where it was coming from. If it was, indeed, getting louder, the source was very probably in front of them. But turning their heads to the forest behind them, the sound seemed just as loud.

"It's the trees," Bill said. "Noise gets kind of lost."

After a minute, Beebe went on about the mules. "Maybe Beverly would help us with the cost."

Greg shook his head. "I wouldn't want to ask him. After footing all the expenses for the expedition, it doesn't seem right to hit him with a thing like that."

"I don't know," Bill said. "If you got a good picture of Bigfoot, he's going to sell a lot of papers."

"Sure," Greg said. "And I suspect Associated Press would pay a pretty good chunk of money for it. But until I develop the film, I don't even want to think about it."

Beebe looked around. "I wonder where Bigfoot is. Do you suppose he could be following us?"

"I don't know," Greg said, thinking for a moment about the barking sound. But then he began to smile. "Well, if the trip has accomplished nothing else, I've got a couple of converts."

"Not me, you don't!" Beebe protested. "Sure, the mules were chased off, and our camp was torn up. But I don't know what did it. It's just easier to say Bigfoot than go around calling it *Something* or *It* all the time. Show me a good picture, and I'll carry a sign down Main street that says I Believe in Bigfoot. Until then . . . well, I still say it's a weird idea, a bunch of giant apes running around in the woods."

Greg grinned at him. "Maybe. You've got one thing wrong, though. Bigfoot is an anthropoid, but not an anthropoid ape . . . the footprints aren't apelike. And what's so weird about it? You don't think deer are weird or rabbits. There are a lot of animals living in the forest and mountains. Why not a two-legged kind? It doesn't violate any law of science, unless you expect it to eat rocks and breathe fire. There isn't a single reason why Bigfoot should be impossible or even unlikely."

Beebe shrugged. "Could be. But when you talk about something being ten feet tall, that's right out of a fairy tale."

"I feel the same way," Greg admitted. "But that's what some of the print and stride measurements have indicated. And when you stop to think about it . . .

105

well, all I know is that the thing that knocked me out sure blocked out an awful lot of moonlight!"

Their discussion came to a halt. As if some kind of wall had been peeled away, the roaring sound had very quickly become louder.

"It's water," Bill said. "A lot of it and moving fast."

"Waterfall?" Beebe suggested.

"Maybe. The map show anything, Greg?"

Greg pulled it out of his jacket pocket and ran a finger along the way they had gone that day. "Nothing . . . unless it's the South Fork of the Smith River. But it's . . . let's see . . . from where we started this morning to the river looks like nine or ten miles. I don't think we could've gone that far."

"No." Bill came over and looked. "Six or seven at most . . . puts us about here." He indicated the border between the Klamath and Six Rivers National Forest. "But maybe that's what we're hearing . . . sure! We've been climbing slowly for the last half hour or so, and now we're at the top where we can hear it better. The Smith is still a mile or two away."

"That loud?" Greg asked.

Bill nodded. "Could be rapids. And I don't know how widespread that heavy rain was, but the river could be up."

As they proceeded downward again, the voice of the river faded once more to the whisper that it had been. It was not until sundown, when the boys started looking for a likely place to camp, that they caught their first glimpse of the Smith through the trees ahead of them.

"That's where we'll stop," Greg decided.

"Yeah," Bill said. "And I think we're going to be there for a while."

Coming out of the trees, they found the Smith very nearly at flood stage. Any attempt at crossing it would be suicidal.

Noting the dismal but quiet way Beebe and Bill stood there staring at the river, Greg shrugged his pack off and got the camera.

"Don't move," he told them. "Stay like that."

"Want us to smile pretty?" Bill asked, wryly.

"Hardly," Greg answered and got the picture.

The boys built a fire on the bank and cooked a supper of canned meat and then wrapped themselves in the tarp to sleep. When the tenth morning came, they could not see any difference in the river.

Sit down and wait it out . . . that was all they could do. There was no way of going around and past the river without spending too much time and winding up even farther from home. And so they made the most of it, relaxing and enjoying the sun. It was good to be away from the shadows and to hear something besides their own voices.

But the tenth day went, and still they had not detected any change in the river. Curious and with growing concern, Bill cut a length of willow and jammed it into the ground right at the edge of the water.

On the eleventh morning, the willow stick was high and dry; the water's edge had moved back a few feet.

But the river did not seem noticeably lower and crossing it was still out of the question.

"Don't know why it isn't dropping faster," Bill said. "Unless the rain lasted longer to the north of where we hit it."

"Maybe it'll look better by tonight," Greg said with tentative optimism.

"What's the big worry?" Beebe asked drowsily. "We allowed for extra time when we packed the food. We aren't in trouble yet."

"Maybe not, *if* we can cross tomorrow and get going." Bill spoke quietly. "If we can't, our margin for error is gone. We'll be using our supplies without any distance to show for it. I don't know how this is going to sit with you guys, but I'm all for buying back a day."

Greg looked at him. "Meaning what?"

"Meaning we drink a lot of tea today. But we don't eat. Okay?"

Something in the young Modoc's voice kept Greg from protesting the idea. Even Beebe did not argue with it.

And so they had strong tea for breakfast and stronger tea for lunch, and tea again that night, sitting around the fire. The day did not pass uncomfortably, but it was unsettling to be reduced to such a thing. It was a warning that nagged at them more than hunger did.

When they turned in for the night, each of them listened to the river and did not hear any lessening of its voice. But then, behind that voice and almost lost, came another sound . . . like an echo of something remembered in sleep.

"He's back," Bill whispered.

Greg nodded and sat up. "Can't tell how far away . . . river's too loud. Can you?"

"No . . . can't figure the direction, either."

"What're you guys talking about?" Beebe came up on his elbow. *"Who's* back?"

Greg glanced at Bill with uncertainty. But the Modoc seemed resigned to it and said, "Might as well tell him."

"The thing that barks," Greg explained. "What Bill and I heard in the last camp."

"Oh, is that bad?" Beebe seemed calm enough, until a shiver betrayed him. "I mean . . . well, what happens now?"

"Don't know," Greg said, "because we don't know what it is. Nothing happened last time, but . . ."

"But if it's the same one," Bill said it for him, "then it *followed* us here. And that, for sure, is something a fox wouldn't do."

"Come on!" Beebe protested. "You aren't going to tell me that's Bigfoot we're hearing!"

"Might be." Bill strained to listen. "You figure it . . . something chases the mules off, and after we're gone, wrecks everything in sight. That night, we hear something that doesn't act like any animal I know, and now we're hearing it *again!*"

"Maybe . . ." Beebe started and then fell silent.

"Take it easy," Greg said. "Nothing happened last time."

"I'm all right . . . not exactly relaxed, but I'm okay," Beebe told him. Then, rather hopefully, he said, "Maybe it's a bear."

"Maybe." Greg went along with it, trying to ease the tension.

But Bill was impatient. "Bears don't bark! And even if they did, there's no reason for one to follow us."

"Sure there is." Beebe pointed at the packs. "Food!"

Bill stepped away from the fire, leaving Greg to state the obvious. "All our food is in cans, Beebe. It can't be smelled, and we haven't even cooked any today."

Beebe took a deep breath. "Okay, so maybe something is following us around, and *maybe* it's Bigfoot . . . are we just going to sit here?"

"It's too dark to move camp," Greg reminded him, "and it might follow us anyway."

"I see . . . nice. Real nice!"

Returning to the fire, Bill said, "If we can get across the river tomorrow, maybe he won't want to follow us bad enough to get wet. Tonight we collect more wood and take turns keeping watch. A bright fire ought to do it."

Beebe nodded. "We don't know what's out there . . . might be Bigfoot . . . might be bad news . . . and now we're going to run around in the big black forest and gather wood? Thanks a lot."

The Indian managed a faint grin. "We stick to the river bank and keep the fire in sight. There's plenty of wood. Won't take long, but you can stay here if you want."

110

"No, you guys need company!" Beebe laughed, a little too loudly. But as if he was just then aware of how he had sounded, he turned quiet and said, "It'll be better if I've got something to do."

A half hour of scavenging along the water's edge produced more than enough wood to last the night. Two-hour watches were decided upon, and Greg took the first. They were tired enough now to settle down and relax. Even Beebe was not as brittle as before; hard work and the simple passing of uneventful time had taken the edge off his nerves. But it took awhile to break the habit of listening. Bill was first to sleep, and in spite of himself, Beebe drifted off a few minutes later.

For a while, as Greg sat there alone, the barking seemed to come closer. And for a short interval, it even stopped. When that happened, he shifted his position and sat with his back to the fire and the river. And watching that first line of trees, barely within reach of the firelight, it was easy to imagine something moving there. But somehow the shadows never turned solid or found definite form, and turning the vigil over to Bill, Greg crawled under the canvas and took his turn at sleeping . . .

16.

The next morning found the river quite noticeably down. It was obvious even without a willow stick to record the difference, and the boys did not have to talk as loud to make themselves heard. The color of the water was also changing; in another day or two, it would probably run clear and sparkling again.

But Bill West looked at it and shook his head. "It's still too high."

"Can't argue with that," Greg said dismally. "But there ought to be something . . . seems stupid to be stuck here. And I don't like spending another night on this side. Not if something's followed us."

"Well, there are ways. If there were about fifteen of us, we could make a chain. And if we had a long rope and a strong swimmer, we could stretch a safety line across. But that's all we've got . . . *ifs.*"

Greg sat down and stared at the fire. "It's my fault.

I should've allowed for the rain. If I'd taken us more to the north when we first started for home, we could've gone around the river."

"Forget it," Bill told him. "The map doesn't tell you how big the Smith is here. And a hard rain *doesn't* always mean high water. How high it gets depends on a lot of things . . . where it rains, how much and how long it's been since the last rain. Sure, I suppose professionals would've pulled out their weather charts and slide rules and magnifying glasses and figured a better way to go. But we can only guess at it."

"Yeah," Beebe quipped. "We're just ignorant kids."

Shrugging, Bill said, "It's true. We didn't know, so we did the simple thing . . . picked the shortest way home. And unless you want to go straight across every mountain, it shouldn't make any difference if you bend a little to the north or to the south."

Greg nodded. "Okay, you've made your point. But we're still in trouble."

Bill opened a pack. "Let's have some breakfast. And then . . . I've got an idea."

"It's all right with me." Beebe grabbed a pot and the can opener. "But what about lunch and supper? I want to know if I should be wild about breakfast or simply ecstatic."

"If my idea works," Bill explained, "we eat lunch and supper. If it doesn't . . ."

"Yeah, I know," Beebe said. "Tea!"

They heated a can of pork and beans and settled down to enjoy it.

113

Feeling better, Greg sighed and looked at Bill. "What's your idea?"

The young Modoc, who had been studying the ridges to the north and south while he ate, pointed downstream. "I'm going to take a walk . . . see if the river widens."

"Don't you want us to go along?" Greg asked, thinking Bill was behaving strangely.

"No." Bill got his knife and cut a six-foot length of willow. "You stay with the food and keep the fire going. See you later." And with that, he left.

"What's with him?" Beebe wanted to know.

"Beats me. I guess it makes sense to stay with the supplies, since we don't know what was making the noise last night. But I don't know why he wants to see if the river widens."

Beebe stood up. "Want me to follow him?"

"No . . . I guess he knows what he's doing."

It was almost three hours before they saw Bill again. He came around some trees along the river and walked toward them slowly. He was obviously tired and his clothes were damp. He did not say anything until he had taken his boots off and settled by the fire to dry his socks.

"Okay . . . I've been across. About a mile and a half below here the river's wide enough to make a difference. Let me rest for a few minutes and then we can take off. I'm a little bushed."

"So I see," Gregg said. "I don't know why we all

114

didn't go. Doing it this way has you walking almost five miles and crossing the river for a third time. You won't be able to make it through the day."

"I'll manage," Bill said quietly.

Watching Bill stretch out and then glancing out across the Smith, Greg suddenly realized why Bill had gone alone. No matter how or where Bill had done it, crossing the river would have had to be a risk. To be *certain* that it could be done, it had to be tried, and rather than argue or gamble with two other lives, he had gone himself . . . all that so they would not go hungry on the way home. Greg was touched by it and grateful for his success . . . and angry because it was a foolish thing to do. He started to say as much, but Beebe beat him to it.

"You know, one of these days, you're going to wind up on a totem pole making a face with the rest of your ancestors! You crazy Indian . . ."

Bill shrugged. "I know me. I do better if I don't have to worry about anything but myself. And it wasn't as bad as you're making it. What do you think the piece of willow was for? A walking stick? I never took a step without first seeing how deep it was."

Greg took a deep breath. "Okay. But why a wide part of the river? Seems to me it would make crossing that much harder."

"Talk about crazy Indians . . . I don't know how your people ever made it from the east coast. It's simple. Where a river widens enough and runs level, it slows down. And when it slows down, it drops the sand and

115

rocks it's been carrying . . . so it's often shallower there. Okay? Now let's get going."

"Don't you want to eat first?" Beebe asked.

"No, let's cross the river and then eat on the move," Bill said, getting up. "We've lost too much time as it is."

The three reached the widening of the river perhaps two hours later. Bill had marked the exact location of his crossing with the willow pole, and they stood there studying the water and the distance.

"All right, now listen," Bill told them. "It hit me around the middle most of the way, and there's enough current to make it a little tricky staying on your feet. But if you lean into it and take it slow, it's not too bad. The worst is toward the center . . . the water came almost to my shoulders there, and I had to swim a few feet before I could walk again. But you two are a lot taller than I am, and so you ought to have less trouble."

"Maybe so . . ." Greg tried to see it in his mind.

"Looks okay," Beebe decided. "Except for one thing, Bill. I can't see you making it with a pack."

"The packs are lighter now," Bill reminded him.

"I know that. But you're built too low to the ground, and when the water starts pulling on the pack, it's going to weigh a ton!"

"He's right," Greg said. "Better make it into two packs."

Beebe was obviously impatient. "And you're going

to hold your camera stuff *and* half of the cans over your head?"

"Only at the middle," Greg replied. "What's wrong with that?"

"No good," Beebe pronounced. "It'd be bad enough to drown five hundred dollars worth of camera and lenses. But our whole reason for going on this expedition in the first place is all wrapped up in that little plastic bag. You're not going to take a chance on losing the film or getting it wet!"

"Hey, Bill," Greg muttered, "the jolly pale giant's getting bossy!"

"Yeah," Bill agreed. "Except he's got a point."

Greg shrugged, liking the whole idea less and less. "Well, I don't know what else to do . . . except make an extra trip."

"No," Bill said. "I found going over and coming back bad enough. Two trips means crossing three times . . . and don't forget, I've had a little rest."

"Well, maybe that's the answer. Beebe and I get the food over. Then I come back, catch my breath and come across with the camera and film."

"That's not the answer and you know it," Beebe insisted.

"What you're driving at," Bill said quietly, "is making one pack of the food, and *you* carrying it. Right?"

Beebe went and stood between them. Making a point of looking down at the tops of their heads, he said, "What could be more logical?"

And it did make sense. In one pack, the food would

117

be heavier than what each of them had carried out of the Klamath. But it would be for only a hundred and fifty feet or so. And someone as tall as Beebe would find it easier to cross the deep part of the river.

Still, Greg objected. "Let's be honest, Beebe. Every time we hit a bad situation, you lose your head. Seems to me if we load you down like that, you have a bigger chance of getting into a spot you can't handle."

Though clearly stung by Greg's candor, Beebe did not give up. "Sure, rattlesnakes scare me. And a maniac with a gun. And the idea of a monster sneaking up in the dark. But this is different. I think you're making too much out of it."

"He's right, Greg. It's tricky, sure . . . but not *that* bad."

"Listen, Greg, for once, being a beanpole is good for something besides basketball! And give me a little credit for brains. I plan to follow you two, so I can see what's coming and be ready. And if I don't like what I see, I can go back. Okay?"

Beginning to see how important it was to Beebe, Greg turned to Bill. "Well . . ."

The Modoc nodded. "That's the way we'll do it."

And so it was settled. The packs were rearranged. Greg had the camera gear and film. Bill took the tarp and what little cooking gear they had. And Beebe inherited the canned goods.

Greg looked them over and said, "Bill, if that tarp causes trouble, get rid of it. The cooking gear, too. All we really need is the can opener."

118

"I don't think I've got enough to bother me."

"Small but wiry," Beebe said, sarcastically.

"We're ready then. If it's okay, Bill, I'd like to go first."

"Pictures?" The Modoc was apprehensive.

"All I need is about a half-minute head start."

"All right . . . but you pick a tree on that bank and use it as an aiming point."

Greg chose one and stepped into the water. It was a shock at first, the cold, fierce tug of it rising toward his waist. But after a few yards, he learned to measure his steps and to lean against the current, aiming a little upstream of where he wanted to go. Taking a last glance back, he saw the others entering the water.

Maybe halfway to the center, a round rock gave way under Greg's foot, and letting out a cry, he almost went under.

"Don't straighten up!" Bill yelled. "And don't stop! You're coming to the deep part!"

After several yards and with growing uncertainty, Greg reached deep water. He wanted to stop and think . . . not just keep pushing this way. It was like stepping toward an edge, knowing he was going to fall and not being able to prevent it. But there could be no hesitation in that current. Using one arm for balance and the other to hold the pack high, Greg charged through with short, hard lunges. He swallowed a little water, and choking on it, moved blindly for a moment. But with a few steps more, the water began moving back down to his waist.

He was tired now, and it was more than luxury to feel the river relinquishing its grip. His legs were heavy and wooden when he stumbled out to dry ground. But he got the camera out and turned in time to catch Bill swimming across the center. Beebe was just now reaching deep water.

That scene was worth a half-dozen shots. Greg watched Beebe through the viewfinder as he moved resolutely through the center . . . and then decided to use the 135mm lens to bring him in closer. But during the switch, he heard Bill cry out.

"Stop! Go back!"

Greg did not see any reason for it. Indeed, Beebe was doing better than they had and only glanced at Bill, as if to say, *take it easy . . . I'm okay.*

But the Indian charged toward him, pointing wildly upstream, shouting, "The *limb,* Beebe! Go back! There's a limb coming!"

Greg spotted it then, saw it riding the current half submerged. So did Beebe, but it was too late. The limb was not very thick, an ordinary casualty of some wind to the north. But it was long, heavy with leaves and full of the river's force. Caught by its impact and entangling branches, Beebe lost his balance and went under.

It was a very long time, a numbing and helpless time of forgetting how to breathe before they saw him again. Beebe came thrashing to the surface a good forty yards downstream. Blinded and strangling, he swam into the

120

shallows and staggered ashore. The pack of food was gone.

When Bill and Greg reached him, Beebe was sitting at the river's edge, crying. But he remained in the distance of his anguish and would not see or acknowledge them. The best they could do was sit with him and wait until the thing began to exhaust itself. And when words finally came, there was nothing in them that had not been guessed. When Beebe had gone under, the pack's weight became too much for him, and he could not come up. Very simply, it was get rid of the pack or drown.

Beebe looked at them wildly with reddened eyes. "Maybe . . . if we search . . . along the bank . . ."

Bill shook his head. "No, it's gone."

"I'm sorry," Beebe mumbled it at them and almost collapsed again. But something close to anger came into his face, and he straightened up. "It *wasn't* panic! You've got to understand that!"

"We know . . . and don't blame yourself," Bill said. "One of those things. It happened and that's that. The best we can do now is get off our rear ends and start walking."

In a little while, they were on their way. And it was easy to look back and find alternatives to what they had done . . . such as waiting another day. At worst, it would have found them running short on food and going hungry for a day or two before reaching Middlefork. But what good was hindsight?

The only thing that mattered now was that they were without food. And with that fact came an ugly ghost to haunt them . . . the possibility of not making it home, ever.

17.

They did not indulge in the luxury of looking for hopeful solutions. The facts were very hard and very clear. They were in a harsh and demanding wilderness where distance could not be measured in the usual way. Elsewhere, twenty or thirty miles might be no more than a day and a half's walk. Here, without food, it was space and time enough to die . . .

It was true, of course, that they had only to turn around and cross the river again and backtrack for ten miles to regain their last camp site on the original route. There, as instructed, they could devise a signal and wait for rescue. And it was also true that they had left, at that camp, a few canned goods. But once there, it would mean waiting five days for the search to begin . . . and they could be there for a longer time, if fog or another freakish spell of rain closed down around those mountains. And so they decided against going back.

It was just not worth it to risk the river again, to spend a hungry night on the way, to reach the camp in an exhausted and weakened condition, and sit around for all those days and nights trying to exist on spoonfuls of apple sauce and fruit juice . . . not when, by traveling just a few miles farther in the opposite direction, toward *home,* they might be able to reach the fire-lookout tower north of Devil's Gap.

The boys were not unaware of the possibility, especially after so much rain, that the tower might not be manned. But if it was not, and they found no food stored there, a permanent lookout station was only a few miles away. The trick, very simply, was to cover the distance . . . *get there.*

And so they had continued on from the river and made the slow and unavoidable climb to the Blue Ridge. There, with Ship Mountain looming to the west, they found the faint trace of a Forest Service trail and turned north toward Hurdygurdy Butte. After three miles, when the trail no longer coincided with their course, the boys located a feeder stream dropping off to the west. This they followed down to Quartz Creek. It was getting dark by then, and they stopped to build their fire for the night.

Considering all that had happened to them that day, the three knew they had done well. They were five miles closer to home, not bad for a half-day's journey. Perhaps the fact of it should have inspired at least some frail spirit of optimism. But it was hard to build a fire and know only its warmth and brightness. This soon, with so far yet to go, hunger was already sharp and strength a failing thing. A hard, wild country was quickly taking its price . . .

Lapsing into wishful thinking, Beebe said, "You know what we should've brought on this trip . . . *flares*. The kind you shoot from Very pistols. Might've saved us a lot of walking. You can see them for miles."

"Yeah, sure." Greg almost laughed. "Especially after it starts a fifty-thousand-acre forest fire!"

"Didn't think of that . . ." Beebe mumbled.

"I know how you feel," Greg said, and then gestured bitterly at the forest around them. "Well, at least we don't have to worry about our barking friend."

"Not yet, anyway," Bill said.

Beebe groaned, "Man, you're a real comfort to have around!"

"He's probably gone, all right," Bill said. "I was just thinking . . . if it was Bigfoot, and he's eight or ten feet tall, crossing the river would be like wading a creek for him."

"Like I said, a real comfort."

Bill stretched out. "I said *if*. And we *aren't* hearing it. So relax."

It was difficult the next morning to get up and face the reality of forcing their way across the necessary miles. They were desperately hungry and sat there staring . . . as if, by magic, some answer to it could be ex-

125

pected of stones, trees and that first thin sunlight. But finally, dismally, they filled their stomachs with water and silently began to walk.

Greg led them along the Quartz for a mile. It forked then and became Jones Creek, and they followed it west past Table Mountain. Their pace was slow, almost listless, but steady. The water kept their stomachs from hurting, but hunger was a sickness in which they could feel themselves slowly fading, dying. It was as if they were bleeding from invisible wounds.

They had gone perhaps three miles when, off to their right, a doe and a four-point buck went springing away. The buck stopped at the top of a rise little more than a hundred yards from the creek and watched them go by.

"That's a lot of lamb chops," Beebe muttered.

Greg nodded. "I'm sorry we decided against bringing a rifle."

"Bigfoot probably would've tied a knot in it anyway," Beebe said. "But it seems like we should be able to do something. Bill, you ought to know about this kind of thing."

"Me? What kind of thing?"

"Finding food . . . living off the land . . . I mean making snares and fishing with a spear . . . making a bow and some arrows . . . what kind of plants can be eaten . . ."

"Why should I know that?" Bill asked.

Beebe shrugged. "Well, you're an Indian."

"Yeah . . . pure reservation Modoc! You sure get funny ideas. When your ancestors put my people on a

126

few acres of land and told them to stay there, they began
to forget how to live. I've never shot an arrow in my life.
Never made a snare or used a spear. I've gone fishing
. . . with a twenty-dollar pole and reel. Indian . . .
you know what I'm good at?"

Sorry that he had brought it up, Beebe said, "No."

"Throwing rocks!"

"Okay, okay." Beebe stopped watching the deer.
"But it seems like we ought to try."

"I know," Bill told him. "And if we had a hundred
miles to go . . . or even fifty . . . that'd be one thing.
But it takes time and energy to make a bow and arrows
and to learn how to use them, and *then* you have to
hunt. I don't know about snares . . . a spear would
be easy, but using it is something else. No . . . the way
I see it, as close as we are to that tower, we're better off
concentrating on just getting there."

"Makes sense to me," Greg agreed.

The logic of it was good . . . to set a goal and not
let it be put aside by other things. By that evening or
tomorrow morning, if they did not have to climb too
much, the tower should be in sight. But logic did not fill
the stomach or nourish, and as the day grew older, their
passage through that bitter landscape took them closer
and closer to delirium . . .

For a long time that afternoon, they had been moving through a deep, tree-buried canyon. The boys had
not minded losing the sun; the day had been quite
warm, and the nearly endless twilight of the redwoods

felt good. But when they came out into more open country, the sun was low, and behind them . . .

It took a few minutes for the fact to register, and Bill was first to notice. "We're headed wrong."

Greg stumbled to a stop and said, "It's just the way the creek bends here."

"But look how late it is . . . we should've turned away from Jones Creek long before now . . . and look at that mountain in front of us."

"We've been going slow," Greg explained.

"*No*, Greg, look at that mountain . . . at the top of it! We've seen it before . . . yesterday."

Greg stared at it, and then something dawned . . . he looked at the map and traced back to where they had been yesterday afternoon. "Lord!" he almost shouted. "That's Ship Mountain!"

"Meaning . . ." Beebe began, "we've been going in a circle?"

Greg looked back at the map, trying to see it clearly. He closed his eyes for a moment and tried again, and then the truth was obvious. "Yes . . . a circle . . . we're only a couple of miles from where we got on that Forest Service trail yesterday."

"That means," Bill said, "we won't see the tower this afternoon . . . and not in the morning, either."

Beebe sat down. "But *how* . . ."

"I don't know," Greg admitted. "As near as I can tell from the map, we've gone two or three miles too far. As Bill said, we were supposed to leave Jones Creek . . . couple of feeder streams leading off to the right

128

toward Fox Ridge. We wanted the second, but I remember seeing only one and that's all. Probably the one we needed. It doesn't help to apologize, but I'm sorry."

"Not your fault," Bill assured him. "It's happened to me a couple of times. Beebe, too. Blanking out . . . staring at nothing . . . and not knowing how long it lasts or where we've been."

It went without saying that such a thing could not be allowed to happen again. Already it had cost them dearly; the seriousness of their situation had been compounded. They had gone miles and hours out of their way . . . distance and time that for the most part would have to be recovered the next day. And by then, they would have had all the long hours of darkness in which to grow weaker . . .

Greg took a deep breath. "Well . . ."

"Let's go," Bill said. "Beebe?"

Beebe could only nod.

They put Ship Mountain to their backs and managed less than a mile before darkness caught them.

18.

When dawn came, the boys did not respond to it but shivered with cold and hunger and fought to go on sleeping. Only when the sun rose and struck at the reddened, crusted lids of their eyes, did they stir and acknowledge the fact of that day. But if earlier they had fought to avoid reality, it was now a struggle to enter into it and function. Not since the seventh night of the expedition had there been a full, unrationed meal. Their last food had been a can of beans two days ago, and even that had followed a day of precautionary fasting. The effects of starvation were rapidly becoming more and more profound.

Greg managed to regain a certain clarity of mind by dashing icy creek water in his face and drinking deep. Bill drank his fill, and though still trembling, was grimly ready to do his best. Beebe seemed to be the worst off. Maybe it was because on that long skinny frame he had less fat to burn. It took awhile to get him up and moving.

Walking slowly, as if half asleep, the three moved deeper into the darkened forest. And it was a little like seeing shadows of themselves coming this way the day before. Few things could have been more discouraging . . . to regain with sleep a feeble and faltering current of strength . . . to get up, somehow, and actually *walk* . . . and know that that precious spark of energy was being spent, not on new ground, but on yesterday's mistake.

It took a good part of the morning to reach the small feeder stream where the error had been made and put Jones Creek behind them at last. From there they had to climb slowly for a mile to the top of Fox Ridge.

"This is bad news," Bill said after the first hundred yards. "Doesn't the map show a better way?"

"Surrounded on three sides . . . Fox Ridge and Blue Ridge join," Greg explained. "Yesterday would've been easier. Gradual slope . . . it's just us. We'll have to take it in stages."

"Wait a minute," Bill told him. "Stop . . ."

"Few more minutes," Greg insisted, "then rest."

"No . . . it's Beebe."

Greg looked back. Beebe had fallen behind and was sitting with his knees drawn up, staring at the ground.

"Beebe?" Bill went down to him. "What's the matter?"

It took Beebe a moment to drift back from wherever it was he had gone. "What . . . ?"

131

Bill shook him gently. "You all right?"

Beebe looked toward the ridge without really seeing it. "Can't make it," he whispered. "Why don't you guys just go on?"

"Not a chance," Bill told him.

That quiet quarrel between strength and apathy struck something in Greg's mind. Without alerting them, he backed off a few feet and started working with the camera.

"It's no good," Beebe sobbed. "Nothing left . . ."

"There's always *something* left. All you got to do is try."

Beebe did not respond, and in the silence Bill heard the camera. Anger flashing into his face, he stood up. "For God's sake, don't you see what's going on! Put that stupid camera away and *help!*"

Surprised, more at himself than Bill, Greg covered the lens and joined them. "Sorry. I . . ."

"It's no good, Greg." Beebe did not even look at him. "I can't do it. Tell this crazy Indian . . ."

"That's silly." Greg got down on his knees. "We'll be resting every few minutes, as much as it takes to reach the ridge."

"Listen, the other day you yelled at me for crossing the river . . . said I was going to wind up on a totem pole with the rest of my ancestors. Well, maybe it was crazy. But you're even crazier if you just give up." Bill hesitated and tried to grin. "Six foot three . . . you trying to be the whole pole?"

132

"Come on, Beebe." Greg nodded toward the ridge. "It isn't so far."

"You can make it easy," Bill said.

Beebe managed a smile. "Indian speak with forked tongue."

"Try me. Come on."

After a minute or two, Beebe groaned and got to his feet. And little by little, they went on.

It was early afternoon by the time the three gained Fox Ridge. There was another Forest Service trail here, but it was going in the wrong direction. After resting for a while, the boys started down the other side of the ridge, following a stream that would take them to Hurdygurdy Creek.

Just a few yards down that slope, Bill let out a yell and pointed at the undergrowth beneath a small stand of Douglas fir.

Greg stopped. "What's the matter now?"

"Berries!"

Hurrying after him, Greg and Beebe finally saw what he had pointed at. Small, dark berries . . . not very many, but nonetheless tantalizing. Beebe immediagely grabbed one and started to eat it, but Greg stopped him.

"Are they all right?" he asked Bill. "I mean, some things like this are poisonous."

"They're okay." Bill showed them stems where berries had already been taken. "Birds. Didn't leave us much."

Beebe picked a few and popped them into his mouth. "Sour . . . bitter . . . delicious!"

Greg and Bill followed suit, and the three of them soon stripped the shrub of its fruit. Looking around, they found two more places where the berries grew and ate all that they could find. Beebe wanted to search for more and so did Greg, but Bill shook his head.

"If there were a lot of berries, it'd be all right, but we're working too hard to get any good out of them. Let's get going."

Greg saw the truth of it and turned back toward the stream. He supposed that, all told, each of them had eaten no more than a handful of the berries.

"But you got to admit," Beebe said, "it sure was nice having something to chew and swallow!"

It was easier, of course, going down. They reached Hurdygurdy Creek after a while and went west along its banks for a quarter of a mile. Then, where a thin stream fed into the Hurdygurdy, they bent their way north to begin climbing again.

There had yet to be any sign of the tower. And as if out of fear of making it go wrong, of putting a jinx on what they wanted, each had refrained from speaking of it. But now the sun was almost down, and they faced the stark fact of spending another night without an answer. And all the mountains were empty . . .

"Maybe the tower's been torn down," Beebe mumbled. "Be just our luck."

134

"The map's too new," Greg told him.

"Well, where is it, then!" Beebe came close to anger. Bill grunted with what was at least a good imitation of impatience. "Why don't you guys shut up! The tower has to be here somewhere. We probably spent more time than we thought picking berries. We just haven't gone far enough, that's all."

But not seeing it was as good, in their hearts, as not believing it could be anywhere within their reach.

When evening came, they were weaker than ever and not at all certain that they could manage another day. And the darkening hour also found them deep in a box canyon. They could not see how to go from there. To climb or go back . . . or just stay and let that be the last place they knew . . . the decision would have to wait for morning and whatever was left of them by then.

Lacking the will to build a fire, they could only wrap themselves in canvas and surrender once more to starvation's nightmares . . .

19.

Morning in that dark, timbered notch was hardly more than a fragment of changing blue above them. The sun was up and yet not a part of their sky; the eastern ridge was too immediate and too high. And not even the slightest wind stirred that shadowed quiet. Opening their eyes to it, the boys only stared and did not move.

They had come, perhaps, to the final barrier. Somewhere in the spirit, there was a limit . . . a time when it became pointless to go on trying. But if they had come to apathy, it was also reflected at them from the dark and motionless world around them.

Only when the sun found that fragment of sky and bathed them with brightness did time seem to move. The still air was hot then, and Bill slowly stood up and walked away. For a while Greg only watched the Modoc growing smaller in a deep green that hung beyond sunlight like darkening clouds. It almost seemed best to let it be. And yet . . . remembering a river, he wondered if Bill had reached another . . . a soundless river not for crossing. With a prickling of fear, Greg got up and shook Beebe.

They went after the Indian, following along that little stream which had led them into the canyon so long ago . . . yesterday. And that quiet, endless mile seemed no more than an illusion misting softly across the mind. And maybe it *was* a dream, one too fragile not to shatter in the sudden noise and gaiety of Hurdy-gurdy Creek.

The boys stood there blinking. Without a word, they stumbled in and fell to their knees. It was good to feel it exploding against them, to bury their faces in that icy flow and drink close to drowning, good to crawl back to dry ground and shiver with the sharp reality of cold.

Greg got the map out, hoping to find what had happened, and for a moment did not know how to unfold it. He closed his eyes hard and then returned to that fine tracery of lines. Like a child learning to read, he pushed a finger along the penciled route . . . followed it from the river to yesterday and stopped. It did not make sense. They should have seen the tower, and they should not have wound up in that canyon. Perhaps his mind had failed again, or he had been thrown off by some inadequacy in the map. But no matter the error, he still felt that they at least had to be close. This mountain facing them . . . maybe it *was* the right one . . . maybe what was visible from there was only a lower ridge. He could not, with the map, find anything to either support or weaken the notion. But having followed the Hurdygurdy to the southwest yesterday, he wondered if it would not be wise to change the angle. Greg nodded to himself and put the map away . . . yes, take the opposite direction and turn northwest at the next fork.

His decision made, Greg found the others lying down again. Their eyes were closed. For an instant, he thought about making them get up and act as if they were alive. But it did not really seem to matter very much.

How long he drifted on the edges of sleep, Greg did not know, but the slightest of sounds caused him to open his eyes. It was Bill. He was up on his knees. Greg started to speak, but something about the young Modoc demanded silence. There was a tension in his body . . . a fine trembling, an electricity that shivered through muscles and begged release. Like a tightening coil and with glacial slowness, Bill reached for a rock. His attention was rigidly fixed on something away from the creek . . . a place of bright sunlight.

Greg could not see what it was and neither could he be entirely sure, there in deep shadows, that Bill was not caught in some kind of waking dream, or that he himself had not fallen into illusion. Digging his fingernails into his palm, he dismissed the idea. Bill was oblivious to everything else around him. A fly . . . a

138

green jewel in a random trace of sunlight . . . circled and landed on the back of Bill's neck to walk in its erratic and mindless way. Certainly it tickled, but the Indian seemed unaware or somehow able to ignore it. Had Greg then blinked his eyes twice, he would have missed that final tightening of the coil and its explosive release. Bill's arm was a sudden blur, and the rock shot across that space with the sound of an angry insect. It made a thudding noise, and Bill was on his feet and running. Greg sat up just in time to see Bill end his sprint and stand motionless for a moment over a dead rabbit. And it was not Bill any more, but something very old and more a part of that forest than an ordinary man could be. With quick ferocity, Bill scooped the rabbit up, thrust it skyward with both hands, and screamed his triumph to the sun.

Greg's scalp crawled and Beebe scrambled to his knees, wide-eyed and wondering. "Hey! What was *that?*"

"Bill," Greg almost whispered. "He got a rabbit . . ."

"Rabbit . . . I thought somebody was getting killed!" But then it dawned on him. "You mean we're going to eat?"

Trembling and still rather far away with what he had done, Bill joined them and said, "Kinda small."

"Sure," Greg told him. "But he's fat, and I'm not about to be particular."

Beebe shook his head with disbelief. "That's what I call luck."

"*Luck!* I told you about rocks. When you live on a reservation and don't have much to play with . . ."

Bill began to smile. "Yeah . . . it's luck, all right. Meat on the table!"

"Well, let's don't stand around just talking about it," Greg complained. "I'll get some wood while you skin him out."

"No," Bill said. "Let's go for a walk."

"*Walk!*" Beebe was incredulous. "We've been starving for days, and you . . ."

"Yes, *walk!* The rabbit doesn't mean our problems are over," Bill yelled at him. Then he tried to be more patient. "If we eat it now, we'll walk it off before we can get any good out of it. It's better to wait until we can stop for the night."

"There's a tower around here somewhere," Greg argued. "You yourself said it couldn't be far."

"Sure, but reaching the tower today isn't something we ought to *count* on. Maybe not even tomorrow."

"Why do you say that?" Greg demanded.

"Why? Do you know exactly where we are on that map? We got lost a couple of days ago, and something went wrong yesterday . . . maybe because we're still lost from the first time. We were supposed to spot the tower yesterday, but we didn't. Can you honestly say you're sure this is Hurdygurdy Creek? How do you know we're not one canyon over or two or three? How do . . ."

"All right." Greg nodded his surrender.

Bill seemed almost embarrassed. "Well, I don't like being the bad guy, but that's the way it hits me. We shouldn't count on the tower until we *see* it. Anyway

140

. . . the day's more than half gone. Just a few hours more. We can wait that long."

And so they went on, Greg leading them to the northeast along the creek he thought and hoped was the Hurdygurdy.

How far they traveled for the rest of that day none of them knew. Their pace was too slow, and their position on the map too uncertain to allow a decent estimate. Greg took them up the first fork in the creek, to the left and northwest. It matched what was on the map, but there were many creeks and many forks. When the sun dropped close to the western ridges, they were no more certain than before as to where they had gone.

"What we need to do," Bill decided, "is get out of the trees and up high . . . maybe we could see where we are."

"Who can climb?" Greg asked, bitterly.

"Maybe tomorrow we'll be strong enough," Bill told him.

"Tomorrow," Greg repeated it. "Sure . . ." It was always *tomorrow* . . . and tomorrow was too far away.

Moments later, Beebe stopped. "Something flashed . . ."

Greg turned around. "What do you mean? Where?"

"Back a couple of steps, I guess." Beebe went back and stared off through the trees to his left. "Don't see it . . ."

Bill and Greg studied what little they could see of the distant ridge.

"I don't know what you were looking at, but I sure don't see anything," Greg said.

"Wasn't looking at anything," Beebe insisted. "It was in the corner of my eye, and when . . ."

"*There!*" Bill shouted. "I see it! The tower!"

"Where?" Greg crowded close and tried to see.

Bill aimed with his finger so that Greg could sight along it. "See? From here it's easy to mistake it for a tree."

Greg nodded then. "Yeah . . . yeah, I've got it!"

"Man," Beebe said, "it's so far away."

"Couple of miles," Bill guessed. "I think there's a clearing ahead of us where we can get a better look, but I don't think we're going to reach the tower today."

And so, again . . . *tomorrow.*

The three continued through the forest and after a few minutes, found the suspected edge to it. They left the creek and climbed across a clear slope into a level, grassy meadow. There was a stand of a dozen pines toward the center, and at the place where grass gave way to needles, they stopped.

The boys had a clear view of the tower and its mountain.

"Well, it's there . . . we've found it, and we have something to eat," Greg said.

"Sounds like a celebration," Beebe agreed. "Just think, for the first time in a long time, we eat, we

142

sleep and we'll get up feeling pretty good. And then we'll go to that tower, and the nice man will feed us again and get on his little radio . . ."

"No." Bill had been frowning. "No! Use your head for a change!"

"What's with you?" Greg wanted to know.

"We can't take that kind of chance."

Beebe was perplexed. "What chance? I mean, we've got the rabbit and *there's* the tower!"

"Yeah, *there* it is," Bill said. "A mile and a half or two, in a straight line. But getting across that lower ridge, and counting all the other ups and downs and rights and lefts, call it five. And climbing the mountain won't be easy. Okay? So it's early in the year, and we've had a lot of rain. Maybe the tower isn't manned and hasn't been since last fall. Which could mean there's no food stored there and no radio. Which means going on to the permanent lookout station north of here. It's two miles farther on the map. But how far when it comes to walking it? Five or six?"

"So I lost my head," Beebe said. "Sue me! But we still . . ."

"Wait," Greg interrupted him. "I don't think Bill's said it all, yet."

Bill nodded and looked at the rabbit. "I wish you'd say it, Greg. I think you know."

Greg sighed and sat down. "It's obvious, Beebe. We have to allow for the worst . . . otherwise we could botch it and die out here. Well, the worst is having to go ten miles . . . and I don't think we could make it."

143

"But the rabbit makes the difference!" Beebe said.

"*No!* It's only a little rabbit, Beebe! A few mouthfuls, divided three ways. Don't you see? We have a much better chance of making it, if just *one* of us eats and goes for help."

Beebe was silent for a long time before he finally sagged a little and nodded. "I guess you're right. But . . . man!"

"I know," Greg said. "It'll be rough on the two who stay here. But with any luck at all, there's a man in that tower, and that might mean eating tomorrow anyway . . . the next morning, for sure."

"So how do we decide?" Bill asked. "Draw straws?"

Greg shrugged. "Far as I'm concerned, you're the one who ought to go. If it hadn't been for that fancy rock throwing, we wouldn't have a rabbit."

"Now wait!" Bill protested. "That's got nothing to do with it. And I wasn't thinking about me being the one to eat."

"Didn't say you were," Greg told him. "But that's the way I think it ought to be. If you don't go, then it's between you and Beebe."

Bill smiled. "I guess it's you, Beebe. With a rabbit under your belt, those long legs ought to get you there in nothing flat."

Beebe stared longingly at the rabbit but somehow managed to turn away. "I guess being hungry hit me the hardest . . . you know me . . . looked like a fugitive from a famine before we even started this trip. Dad says I've got the metabolism of a bird, no fat to live on, and you saw what happened. I tried to give up . . . remember? But you, you crazy Indian . . . man, you're right at home out here! You've been the smartest and strongest. I'm beginning to think you can live on air and water, because you're the strongest even now. No . . . I'm staying. The rabbit would be wasted on me."

"But I don't . . ." Bill began. "Okay, so why not you, Greg?" Greg shook his head "I've got a feeling I'd never make it. Beebe's right. You've got the best chance, and there's no point in arguing about it."

And so wood was gathered and a fire started. With a few deft strokes of his knife, Bill skinned the rabbit and impaled it on a green branch. But he did not start roasting the meat just yet.

"Listen," he said quietly, "Let's be sensible."

"I know." Greg turned to Beebe. "You and I better go somewhere else for a while."

They climbed upwind and out of sight. At timber's edge, the two settled down to wait.

Why it came now and not before, Greg did not know, but it was an odd feeling . . . being so *aware* that Bill was eating. And there was no place for it . . . there could *not* be any resentment. Troubled, wondering if Beebe felt the same thing, he turned to his friend and found a strange little smile in his face.

"What've you got to smile about?"

Beebe watched the stars. "I was thinking of all the trouble I've caused . . . complained a lot, started a fight, turned chicken a few times. And even if it wasn't

145

my fault, I'm *still* the guy who lost the food. Some record! Well, maybe tonight I made up for some of it."

"I don't understand . . ."

"You know . . . the rabbit. Deciding I wasn't the right one to eat it. It would've been so easy to say yes . . . and I *didn't*. Well, it's no big deal . . . I mean, even a blind man could see that Bill is our best bet. But I sure feel easier about things."

"It's better than I'm doing," Greg whispered.

"Huh?"

"Nothing."

20.

Greg supposed he had drifted off for only a moment. And yet, suddenly cold, he opened his eyes to see the thin blue light of morning. Startled, he shook Beebe awake, and they tried to hurry down to the fire. But there were only ashes now, and Bill was already gone.

After so many miles together, it felt strange to stand in that empty place. Bill's journey was a hopeful one, it was true, but it was also a matter of having been, for a while, reduced to two. And it was all too clear to both of them, how much they had depended on that quiet little Modoc.

"Wonder how he feels." Beebe sat down trembling and carefully studied the ground around the ashes of Bill's fire.

"Much better, I'm sure."

Beebe drew his knees up and closed his eyes. "Didn't even leave the bones."

"Probably took them with him. For the marrow. He might have a long way to go."

The sun was just beginning to break over the eastern ridges then, and for a long time they watched the land to the west emerging from night's last shadows. But they could not see their friend moving across it.

"Must've left while it was still dark," Beebe observed.

Nodding toward the neatly folded canvas, Greg said, "Early enough for dew to form."

"When do you think he'll reach the tower?"

"Early afternoon, I guess," Greg said, and then added, "He's got to take it slow . . . just in case he has to go on to the permanent lookout station."

"But if there's somebody . . . well, the man in the tower . . . he could be here by dark. Maybe earlier. I think we ought to build a big, smoky fire so he can see exactly where we are."

"Yes, that makes sense. This afternoon we'll build a fire."

But privately Greg did not dare set a time limit to his hopes. Bill was on his way and doing his best, and that was the only certainty. The sixteenth day . . . not a lot of days, and yet it was in some way forever. It was difficult to remember now, with any sense of closeness, home and Middlefork . . . the sounds and smells, the faces . . . the familiarity of a room, a bed, a door that squeaked . . . all the fragments and pieces that added up to life and being part of a place.

Greg stared at the sky until he felt as if he were falling into it. *Let Bill make it.* He silently mouthed the words. *We're dying.* It was strange . . . dying was something that happened to other people. But now it was happening to them. That was what hunger was, even with its first, faint gnawings . . . a warning of it. And so much time had passed.

Later, the two stirred and spent part of the morning in a futile search for berries. Somehow they knew it would be pointless, but looking was better than doing nothing; it had to be tried. When the sun was straight up, they settled down again and watched the tower as if, from that distance, Bill might be seen climbing up the last of that steep mountainside toward the summit. But it was only frustrating, a quiet kind of torture, to sit there and stare until eyes burned and watered. Once, they stumbled down to the creek below them and drank deeply of its cold, sweet water, and then climbed back into the heat of the day to watch the tower again. But they finally gave in to the anguish of endless waiting and crawled into the shade of the pines and there let a fevered half sleep come to them.

Several times, as the afternoon grew older, Greg tried to wake up and move. The fire, he kept remembering, had to be built. But he could not break out of that torpid state until the air turned cooler with sundown.

He shuffled away from the trees and stood there doing nothing . . . his vision was fuzzy and his mind was stuffed with cotton. Only when Beebe joined him did he react with a start and begin to function.

149

"No sign of anyone yet," he said. "Got to build that fire."

Beebe nodded slowly. "A big fire . . . light up the whole hillside. What do you suppose has happened?"

"Don't know." Greg glanced toward the tower and then returned to the trees to look for wood.

It took maybe a full hour, moving as slowly as they did, to get enough wood together and start it burning. And when it burned, leaping six feet into the air and illuminating so much of that clearing, it seemed as if the whole world would have to see its brightness. But it would be only a speck from the tower, Greg knew, and obvious only if someone happened to look their way . . . if there was someone.

If . . . there were too many questions. Maybe Bill had found the tower vacant and was north of it now, headed for the permanent station. But maybe the rabbit had not been enough after all, and Bill had yet to reach the tower. Or maybe he was lying in a canyon somewhere, injured. It simply was not for them to know.

Greg and Beebe had expended themselves to build that hopeful blaze and perhaps it had not even been important. The fire would not last, and as time passed, it seemed more and more obvious that help would not come that night. That was the worst of it, being reduced to helpless waiting. And for how long? That night, another day, or a single hour . . . any measure of time seemed impossible. Beebe was too silent and giving up again, and Greg felt his own will slipping away. The

150

two were like the fire, burning down to the last of existence, and not once in their waiting had they been aware of blindness . . .

The fire had burned low and let the darkness come more closely around them before they could begin to see any distance beyond it, before they could see the larger stars, and after a while, the pale and cosmic frost of the whole Milky Way. Its awesome, glittering sweep only emphasized how small and alone they were; and how, like man from the very beginning, they never entirely belonged to the night and depended on their puny fires to keep it away. Greg lowered his eyes, and for a time watched only those dying flames. But a brighter star, quite low on the horizon, kept intruding on the growing stillness of his mind . . . it seemed to demand that he be aware, that he give it his attention. And staring right at it, Greg slowly began to realize how close it was and how oddly it behaved. The star was not a star at all, but a light signaling from the tower. Bill had made it . . .

21.

The man from the tower reached them shortly after midnight; woke them from bad dreams, fed them well and let them sleep again. Over breakfast at sunrise, the boys were informed that the Six Rivers *Sentinel* had been contacted through the District Ranger Station in Gasquet. The call, in fact, had been made just in time to cancel a search prompted by the ominous sight of two mules returning home alone.

When breakfast was over, and the boys were better able to travel, their rescuer had led them not toward the mountain, the way Bill had gone, but to the north and a lower ridge. There, on the other side, they came to an access road that snaked slowly toward the tower. Had Bill come this way, he would have had to walk two miles farther; enough to cancel out the advantage of an easier climb. But Greg and Beebe were spared that long trek to the summit. Not more than a hundred yards from where they reached the road, they found Bill sleeping in a jeep.

The three were then driven to Gasquet, transferred to a station wagon and taken the remaining eight or nine miles on Highway 199 to Middlefork. Their families were waiting for them, and they were taken to the hospital for examination before being sent home to rest. And with that, the ordeal was over . . .

For a time, Greg had no choice but to surrender to a bed and let the world go away. And sleep was fitful . . . he kept stirring and rising to the surface as if something within still demanded the walking of a needed mile. Perhaps still linked to the cycles of a journey, deep sleep came only when the sun went down.

But late that night, a shadow, a ghost of wilderness crossed, a questioned image came to the edge of his mind and waited until Greg moved and opened his eyes . . . and then was gone. He watched the room in the dark, remembering. Bigfoot . . .

Since his parents were asleep by then and could not object to his being out of bed, Greg took the expedition film into the darkroom. He had looked forward to this moment, and yet it was also a frightening thing to face. Hundreds of times before he had stood in total black and by sense of touch wound film onto the developing reels. And just as many times, with careful attention to minutes and temperatures, he had put film through baths of developer and hypo. It had become automatic and routine. But so much had been endured in order to

153

photograph Bigfoot that it was impossible not to be tense and apprehensive. His hands trembled now as he began the task. One simple mistake could reduce the expedition to a pointless walk.

It was also a time of questions and impatience . . . the two chemicals took a total of thirteen minutes, and during that interval the film and all its images remained a secret inside a stainless steel canister.

Although the darkroom was comfortably cool at that hour, Greg perspired freely during the last minutes of the processing. But finally the film was ready for the water bath, and it was safe to open the can with the light on. Greg rinsed the reels briefly and then held them up, slowly unwinding them against the light to study the water-beaded images. He had not kept the reels in any particular order, and with the background so similar in many of the negatives, he could not remember when or where they had been taken. The general coverage of the expedition looked good, but it held no interest to him yet. He was down to the last reel before he found the frames he was looking for.

And then Greg began to feel sick. Frame after frame revealed nothing more than trees and shadows caught in the brilliance of the flashbulbs . . . yes, and then a few blurred images of *something*. The focus! In the dark, he had not gotten the focus right.

Only in one negative, almost entirely obscured by lunging mules, did he find his target sharply defined. Greg held his breath and tried to be hopeful. It was hard, in that small, wet rectangle of film, to tell what he had. Greg thought he saw what might be an eye, what looked like a hairy arm or foreleg, and a small portion of an area below the arm and toward the rear of the rib cage. But he could not be sure. If would've been easy enough to put the frame on the enlarger and project a much bigger image. However, not wanting to risk scratching it while the emulsion was soft, Greg put the film back into the water.

Having almost an hour to wait after the film was hung to dry, he went back to bed. Greg tried to keep his mind elsewhere by thumbing through some of his old photo magazines. But even the articles on jewel-like lenses, test reports he had almost memorized, failed to pull him away from that impatient hour. Instead, he found himself deciding that he would print all the frames, however bad, on the remote chance that something could be learned from them. But he was grasping at straws and knew it. As for the one good negative, the best that could be said was a cautious *maybe*.

Later when the film was dry, he made contact sheets with all the negatives so that James Beverly could choose the pictures he wanted. That done, he did five-by-sevens of all the bad frames of Bigfoot. As he had feared, they revealed only a blur almost lost in a clutter of trees. If anything could be decided from them, it was simply that the object was quite large and walked upright.

His heart no longer in it, he raised the enlarger and made an eleven-by-fourteen of the sharp negative and again found only what he thought was there . . .

nothing more. The eye was too full of glare from the flash unit to have detail, and the rest of it . . . well, the creature in the photograph could have been Bigfoot, and just as easily, a bear . . .

22.

The following evening, Bill, Greg and Beebe joined Beverly at his house for a steak dinner. They sat through it, trying not to seem disappointed over what to them was an obvious failure. The expedition had accomplished nothing. But the editor was quite aware of what they felt and even seemed a little amused at them in a sympathetic way.

Beverly pushed back from the table and lit his pipe. "Well, it's true the photographs don't shed any light on the Bigfoot question. And your description of what destroyed your camp is vague at best. From that standpoint, the expedition failed. But you tried, and if it makes you feel any better, what you went through still makes a darn good story . . . and one with a nice touch of mystery to it. It should be enough for two or three installments, and I think there's at least a dozen pictures we can use."

Greg stared into his plate. "That's something, I guess. Maybe the real proof of Bigfoot has to wait until somebody manages to actually capture one, but it would've been nice to come back with a good picture. You know, one that couldn't be doubted. I wanted to be first, but I don't think I'd have the courage to try again."

"Ditto," Beebe said, fervently.

Quietly, his eyes full of remembering, Bill said, "I don't know. I didn't like being hungry. But the rest of it . . ."

The editor nodded and supplied the word. "Adventure."

"Yes," Bill said. "That was good."

Beverly got up and, stretching, went to the window to look at the forest across the creek. "You know, I'm glad you didn't succeed in photographing Bigfoot. I guess that surprises you. But while there is something gained in discovery, something is also lost. The moon, for example, mankind has touched it, and that's a wonderful thing. But it's not the lovely mystery that it used to be. And the worst day in man's history will come when he has nothing left to puzzle over."

"I never thought about it that way," Greg confessed. "But . . ."

"I know," Beverly anticipated him. "You went with more than discovery in mind. I haven't forgotten."

Bluntly Beebe plunged in. "Does he get the job?"

"Oh, for crying out loud, Beebe! I'm sorry, Mister Beverly. My idiotic friend has a large mouth!"

Beverly waved it off. "No apology necessary. I was

158

about to broach the subject anyway. I've been thinking . . . I can't hire you as a photographer. Not yet. But I'm willing to let you work on a trial basis for a couple of months . . . call it an apprenticeship. You would be given assignments, an expense account and payment for the pictures I use. Admittedly, it wouldn't be much more than pocket money. However, in return for this, I would teach you as much as I can about photo-journalism. And at the end of two months, if I think you've made enough progress, the job is yours. Fair enough?"

"Yes . . . sure." Greg was dumbfounded. "More than fair! But I don't understand. I mean . . . well, when I applied for the job, I didn't meet your require-ments. And I don't think the expedition shots are so special that they'd change your mind."

Beverly smiled. "No, you're not a great photographer, but you aren't so bad that you can't handle the assign-ments. The purpose of teaching you is that over the long term I need something better. And you're right about the pictures. They aren't what changed my mind. The *idea* impressed me. It showed more imagination than I saw in your portfolio. Then, too, I can't ignore the ambition involved. That's important. No matter how good he is, I don't want a photographer who waits for assignments. In Middlefork, that would mean weeks of nothing better than head shots. Each issue ought to have at least one picture to delight the eye or tell the reader something about himself or the place he lives in. And once a month, regularly, I'd like to have a full-page

159

spread of photographs dealing with some aspect of the people and the region. That kind of thing doesn't grow on trees, as I'm sure you've learned. I think you ought to give it a try. Can you be at the *Sentinel* Monday morning?"

Beebe answered for him. "He'll be there first thing . . . man, like Sunday night!"

J. Allan Bosworth began writing while still a radioman aboard USS *Missouri*. World War II had just ended, and the ship was on her long voyage home. A native Californian, he returned to San Francisco and took a job at the *Chronicle*. Ten years later, having published two novels and a few dozen short stories, he left the newspaper to begin writing on a full-time basis. He and his wife and two daughters now live in Salem, Virginia. Among Mr. Bosworth's previous books for young people are *White Water, Still Water, All the Dark Places,* and *A Wind Named Anne.*

N18